Love carries its own power and healing.

–BLUE SAFFIRE

Clouded Views

Love's Brew Series

BLUE SAFFIRE

Perceptive Illusions Publishing
Bayshore, New York

Blue Saffire/Perceptive Illusions Publishing, Inc
PO BOX 5253
Bayshore, NY 11706
www.BlueSaffire.com

Ordering Information:
Quantity sales. Special discounts are available on quantity purchases by corporations, associations, and others. For details, contact the "Special Sales Department" at the address above.

Clouded Views/ Blue Saffire. -- 1st ed.
ISBN 978-1-941924-40-2

CHAPTER ONE

It's Her

Hershel

I purse my lips in frustration as I look down at my phone. I worked my ass off on this final paper. I'm not going to miss the deadline because of a stupid email glitch.

"Hey, man. You mind if I use your laptop? I was supposed to email my paper in but it's saying it didn't go through, and it won't work in this stupid app. I just want to log in and make sure it gets through on time," I say to Kordell as I stand in his living room going through my emails while I wait for him.

Kordell and I have been friends for years. We grew up in Spring Valley together. He's my best friend.

We do almost everything together. I was so upset when his parents decided to move, and he had to change schools. He was the only friend I had that I knew wanted to be my friend for me.

"Sure. Go ahead."

Sitting at his desk, I then log in and sure enough the draft with my paper is still sitting there. I grumble a curse to myself and make sure the email is sent this time.

Once I'm done, I log out and close the tab. I snort as the web address for the tab Kordell left open comes into view while the page refreshes. I can't believe he's still going through with this.

"Dude, you're still on this site? I thought you changed your mind," I call out.

He comes from his room to see what I'm talking about. I turn to look over my shoulder at him. He shrugs his shoulders.

"I'm on the fence. I mean, look at her. Wouldn't you reconsider?"

I turn to see who he's talking about. My eyes nearly pop out of my head as the page fully refreshes. I flap my mouth open and closes like a fish, not able to find words.

"You have to be fucking kidding me," I finally breathe.

About a year ago Kordell tried to get me to sign up for this website. It's not quite a dating site. Well, it is, and it isn't.

It's a website for women looking for guys to breed with. I thought Kordell had lost his mind at first. My daddy would kick my ass. I'm already keeping a big enough secret from him.

"She's a knockout, right? I couldn't believe it when we matched either. Everything about her is perfect.

"I don't know. I agreed to our first meet but I'm thinking about cancelling. Something has to be wrong with her, she's too perfect," he muses.

"Oh, she isn't but she is. Trust me," I say almost to myself.

JC has been nothing but short with me from the first time we met. She's gorgeous and smart as hell but she doesn't like me for some reason. I have no idea where I went wrong.

"You say that as if you know her," Kordell says.

"I do. This is one of Coral's girls."

"You mean your pop's new girlfriend?"

"Yeah."

"This wouldn't be the one you were all twisted up about, would it?"

"That was Jo. No, I was into Jo until I realized I didn't have a shot and then I met her," I say pointing to the screen.

"In that case, I was right. Something is off. I'm not going to go through with it."

"Um, wait." I stop him from getting ready to cancel their meet. "You don't mind if I go instead of you, do you?"

Kordell looks at me as if I have two heads. I get it, he's Black and I'm white. It's not like I can pass for him or anything. I don't know what I'm thinking, but I need to be the one who shows.

I feel it in my bones. I may not have wanted to sign up to meet some random who wanted to take my baby and ride off into the sunset, but there's something about knowing I could give this to JC.

Not the sex, but the opportunity to have something to smile about. I've seen her smile. She needs to do it more.

"Suit yourself. This better not come back to bite me," he says and reaches to squeeze my shoulder.

"I'm sure it won't. I just want to meet with her and see if she's open to talking this out with me."

"Do you really think that's a good idea? That's like Catfishing or something, man."

"Listen, I'll come up with something. I mean, look at your profile. It reads just like mine would expect for the photo and ethnicity. We could pass for the same person."

"Hersh, buddy, did you bump your head?"

"No, tell me I'm wrong. You're not my best friend for nothing. We're just alike."

"You're forgetting your family is slightly wealthier than mine," he teases.

"Not by much. Besides, none of that will come up. She's not looking for marriage, remember?"

"I know what she's looking for. Do you remember that fact? What do you plan to say to her about that?"

"I don't know. Maybe this is a bad idea."

"I'm sure it is."

"Do you mind holding off on cancelling? Let me think about this. If I don't figure something out, then you can call the meet off."

"Man, I want to meet this girl now. Okay, okay, I'll hold off. I want to hear what you come up with though. It looks like you might need me to save you from yourself."

"Fine, I'll let you know when I come up with something," I murmur.

"Jodie Cadence, pretty name."

"Yeah, she likes to be called JC, but Jodie Cadence suits her."

I begin to think of a master plan. I did start the sign-up process a year ago, I just never finished it. I can't help but wonder if we would be a match if I completed my profile.

Nope, that's a dumb idea, but I would need proof that I'm a safe partner. Yeah, she would need to know that.

Think Hersh, think.

Jodie Cadence

"Oh my, dear, are you all right?"

I blink back the tears threatening to spill. I don't even remember coming here. I've been on autopilot since leaving my appointment.

An appointment I had to face all my fears to attend. Now I wish I hadn't forced myself to do any of it. Ignorance is bliss.

Isn't it?

"Alice, I—" My voice breaks and my words get stuck in my throat.

"Come, come, sit down. Would you like some coffee or hot chocolate? You love the salted caramel brew, don't you?"

I nod unable to speak. Alice has grown on me in the last four months. I find myself coming here a lot to think and decompress.

I need that luxury today. My heart aches so bad. I've wasted so much time, now look. How did I get here?

"JC, honey, what's going on? Talk to me," Alice says once she returns with coffee and a slice of fudge for me.

I shake my head. I don't even know where to start. I haven't told Mom or my sisters what's going on. This latest development makes me glad that I haven't.

When I signed up for that breeding site it had been a joke between me and a few of my girls back home. My friend Kasey had tried it out and now she has an adorable little girl.

Although I check it for matches from time to time. I hadn't truly been serious about going through with it. Now, I don't think I have a choice.

Kordell seems like a great guy. In his thirties, studying to be a doctor, fine as hell from his pictures. However, I have questioned why he's on the site if he's such a great catch. Ha! He's probably thinking the same thing about me.

"Jodie Cadence, you can talk to me," Alice says, pulling me out of my head.

"All my life all I wanted was the opportunity to get it right. Mom and Uncle Ralph showed me what that looked like as parents and as a couple.

"I understood their divorce. I respect them for it. I wanted to find my own time where I could have what they had. I wanted to raise my own babies to know the love they gave us.

"Not the mess I watched my father put my mother through or the love he didn't show up with. I wanted to give what he wouldn't give us. I wanted them to feel wanted.

"My ex made me all the promises, and I was on my way to it all. Then I found out he was cheating with a younger version of me. In one breath he took it all away after wasting seven years of my life.

"First, it was too soon to think about marriage. Then, it was let's focus on our careers and getting promotions. Then, it was he had family things back home to handle when I didn't know there was a back home for five years.

"There was always something. I was so busy working, I didn't see it coming. He proposed to her while still sleeping in my bed."

I pause to shake my thoughts clear. "To be honest, she can have him. I could care less about David.

"I've made my peace with that. What's killing me is I'm losing my window to have a baby. I found out this morning that I have a condition that might make it impossible in another two to three years," I begin to sob.

"Oh, sweetheart." Alice gets up from the seat across from me and comes to sit beside me. "The Lord works in mysterious ways. He will give you the desires of your heart. You will see."

"I hope you're right." I sniffle.

"I know I am. You're a gorgeous, smart, and talented young woman. I'm sure you will find a nice young fella soon enough."

I snort. "I've been too angry to date. Two months ago, was my first session with my therapist. I need to unpack all the garbage for myself before I drag a baby or anyone else into all of it. However, this gives me no time for any of that."

"You have to stop saying that or thinking it. Trust the process. Work on the things you can change now. The rest, allow time for your faith to bring it to you."

"Thanks, Miss Alice I needed to hear that, and I needed to say it all out loud."

Change what I can change now. I pull out my phone and confirm my date with Kordell as well as accepting the extension on my apartment in Kelly. That's where my therapist is.

It's a few towns over from Spring Valley but still far enough for me to keep some privacy for now. I don't want to burden Mom or my sisters with this.

I chose Dr. Catherine because she fit all my criteria. She had great reviews, her practice is run from her home, and she's soft spoken. Besides, Spring Valley inspired me to move in the right direction to seek her out.

I figured I'd find someplace close to it. Kelly is much bigger than Spring Valley and has more of a Metropolitan vibe. The rumor mill isn't as present there, not like Spring Valley and it's close-knit community.

Traveling the world didn't give me the answers I was looking for. Therapy seemed like the next logically step. I have a lot of things I need to address, not just my anger.

My phone rings in my hand and I groan. My supervisor wants me to return to work full time in the office back in the city. I'm not ready for that.

I don't want to look at David's stupid smug face. I'm over him, but that doesn't mean I don't want to punch him in the face every time I see him.

I didn't mean to start dating a guy where I work, but here I am. In my defense, I worked there first. David charmed his way into a position after we met.

Red flag number one. I could kick myself now in hindsight. There were signs way before the end.

"Sorry, Miss Alice, I need to take this."

"You take your time. I'll get out of your way."

She gets up and gives my shoulder a gentle squeeze. I give her a smile, grateful for her allowing me to vent. This place has become a place of comfort since my first visit.

The scent of the fresh bake goods welcomes you in like home. The vibe makes you want to stick around, and Alice is the icing on the cake. She's just adorable.

"Hello," I say as I answer the call.

"Jodie Cadence, I wanted to talk to you about this project. We're very excited and want to see everything you've been working on," Gretta sings on the other end.

"Oh, that's great. I'm already here in Spring Valley. Do you want to set up a Zoom to talk logistics."

"Actually, I have a ton going on here since my best employee is still out of the office." I roll my eyes, knowing she's talking about me. "Can you email me with the latest?"

"Sure, no problem."

"Great. We're sending someone to get you caught up on all the details on our end." She pauses to talk to someone in the background while moving away from the phone.

"Sorry about that. Oh, yes, shoot me an email and we'll talk some more before your team member arrives. Congratulations. I think this is going to be amazing."

"Thanks. Talk soon."

I crack a little smile, happy for some type of good news. For now, I'm going to focus on work and loving myself. Maybe Kordell will turn out to be a good move. Just my luck he could want more than to breed.

That just sounds crazy, Jodie Cadence. Yeah, but what are my other options? This is the only way I can handle right now.

CHAPTER TWO

Replacement Date

Hershel

"I truly can't believe you talked me into this. We both have totally lost our minds," Kordell says to me as we walk into the restaurant he and JC agreed to meet at.

He's right. I think I have lost my mind. I have gone through the entry process to sign up to Meet and Breed.

The physical, the psych elevation, the financial analysis, and background check. They want a lot from someone who's not interested in a real relationship. However, I've done every single step as if I plan to find a match. When in reality, I only plan to swap places with Kordell this evening.

"Just follow the plan. I'll handle the rest," I murmur.

"The plan is stupid. You're not stupid, buddy. Why not tell her you're interested? Why all the games?"

"She's so guarded and I think she's made up her mind about me for some reason. I'm not trying to play games. I'm only trying to step out of the environment she's used to seeing me in in hopes she'll take another look."

"Have you ever thought that maybe you're not her type?"

I frown. "But she connected with you and we're just alike."

"Bro, again with this." He laughs. "Yeah, we have a lot in common, but your ass is and always will be white.

"I can't pass for you, and you could never pass for me. I don't care how many boxes we check that are the same. I think she might be more pissed at the fact that you can't see that. It's giving privilege, bro. It's giving privilege big time."

I groan. "I hear you but I'm here. I understand what you're saying but I've committed to trying this at least."

Kordell sighs. "If you understood you'd turn around and take your ass home." He sighs again. "Well, there she is. If I'm not going to get you to change your mind and leave, let's do this."

I pat him on the back. "Thanks, man. I really appreciate this."

"Yeah, yeah. You're always up to some crazy shit but this takes the cake, but I think I see why. Damn, her pictures don't do her any justice. I might be making a mistake here.

"You're going to fuck this up and you're going to fuck it up for both of us. Why did I agree to this again?"

"Because you're my best friend and I knew her first. Next time you need a wingman, I've got you."

"Yeah, yeah, sure you do. That is if this one doesn't kick me right in the balls. I might not be able to have children at all after this."

"Think positive."

"Hershel? What are you doing here?" JC asks as we walk up to the table.

"My buddy here had some car trouble. He asked me to get him here," I say.

"*Okay*," she drags out. Then she frowns.

"Wait, you know each other? You have to be fucking kidding me. This would be my luck."

"Kordell is my best friend. We've known each other since we were in diapers."

"Yay, so nice for you both. Listen, this feels off so I'm going to take off."

"No, no. Wait."

"I had been looking forward to this meeting and like Hersh said, my car gave out. You seem like a busy woman, and I've had a ton of work and things to focus on.

"It felt like it would be a now or never thing for both of us. I didn't want to miss the opportunity. Hersh only came in because in my rush to get inside, I forgot your roses in the car," Kordell says as he nods to the bouquet in my hand.

I silently thank him for thinking fast. JC looks at the roses then between the two of us. I want to kick myself.

I don't know what I thought was going to happen, but this is blowing up in my face so much faster than I thought. I shake it off and hold out the roses. JC takes them and narrows her eyes.

"So you couldn't hand him the roses and leave?" she says.

"We started taking about our residency and made it to the table before I could finish telling Kordell about the opportunity on the bulletin that he didn't see. It's time sensitive so I wanted to get him all the info," I say, thinking quickly.

JC's brows furrow. "You're a vet. You serve animals. From our talks and his profile, he's a pediatric resident—"

"I told you. We're just alike. Kordell started out as a vet like me. I'm still practicing as a vet but we're both in the same program for pediatrics."

"Wait a minute. I've never heard about this before. The way you're always talking, trying to impress me, why wouldn't you mention this before?"

"Damn," Kordell coughs into his hand.

"I've mentioned it before. I'm sure I did. Maybe you weren't around but I've thrown the idea out there a time or two.

"But to be honest, it's been my secret. I haven't told Pop or Chance. I attended school here in Kelly, my residency has been here as well. It's something I started when mom first got sick. I wanted to finish for her. She passed right before my final year.

I pause and swallows hard. Just thinking about that time places a lump in my throat. Mama and Kordell were the only ones to know I returned to school.

I hadn't known how to tell Pop I had changed my mind about working on the ranch. My dreams were taking me elsewhere.

Mama encouraged me, she's the one who told me I would be fine no matter what.

"I … I haven't told Pop because … it's been hard, and it never feels like the right time. I'm hoping to land this new position in Spring Valley and do a portion of my residency there. Then I can talk to Pop."

JC rolls her eyes. "This isn't what I came here for. I have my own drama. Thanks for coming, Kordell. It's nice to meet you but I'm going to go."

"Jodie Cadence, come on," Kordell croons as he turns on the charm. "I'm starving. Let me buy you dinner at least."

"Does that mean your chaperon has to stay?"

"He's my ride. Since we all know each other maybe I could feed you both for the inconvenience I've caused you guys." He shrugs.

"I don't have to sit with you," I murmur.

"No, go on and sit. I am hungry," JC sighs.

"Great. I just need to head to the bathroom. Order whatever you want, I'll be right back," Kordell says.

He waves a waitress over for us to place our order. I give him a nod of thanks as he leaves, knowing he's not coming back. That didn't go as I planned.

Jodie Cadence

These two aren't pulling anything over on me. I don't know what kind of freaky deeky shit they're on but I'm not into none of that. I sit glaring at Hersh's weird ass.

"So you want to be a pediatrician. How's that working out for you?"

"I love it. Animals are great and I don't think I will ever stop volunteering once I've gotten my pediatric license, but making the little ones feel safe and putting them back together is much more rewarding," he replies.

The way his eyes light up tells me this is truly his thing. I tilt my head to the side and look at him more closely. I'll admit. Hershel isn't bad looking at all. He's actually fine as fuck.

Jack has some handsome sons. Hershel just met me at the wrong time in my life, and I felt some type of way because I could tell he had been sniffing around Jo before I arrived, but his brother sealed the deal before he could.

Besides, I'm not into entitled assholes. I mean, the fact that he's gone from one doctoral degree to the next proves that. How many people can afford to make that decision?

I frown as I realize I can say the same for Kordell. I don't plan to have a real relationship with Kordell. He did state that he doesn't think he wants to be a part of the baby's life but is willing to meet the child in the future if they want.

However, what does that say for his future decisions concerning my child. He could be just as fickle about the child and decide he wants way more or nothing at all. That's not what I want for my baby.

"How did you both end up changing career paths? Are you both indecisive? Is that y'alls thing?"

"No, no. I wouldn't say we're indecisive. I can't speak for Kordell but for me … who knows what they really want at eighteen. All my life I was told that the ranch would be my responsibility someday.

"Don't get me wrong, I love making beer with Pop and Chance. I will always do all I can to keep the place running but I wanted more. Something of my own, you know?

"Medicine has always fascinated me. I went into veterinary medicine because I loved working with the horses. It correlated back to the ranch.

"I just hadn't felt fully fulfilled. Kordell and I were talking about opening a practice together one night and I blurted out the confession of wishing I had gone into pediatric medicine. The rest is history." He shrugs.

"I guess I can understand that. I've questioned my path in the last few years."

"You're great at what you do. The festival you guys put together was amazing."

"Thanks, but my job is way more than pulling together a street fair."

"Pop said something about that. What is it you do again?"

"I'm the executive director of marketing and social media management. I basically design the marketing plan for every project we run. I then make sure the events and projects go viral and produce a return.

"Gaining all the right eyes. Pulling in the right donors and sponsorships. I connect the big dots and bring in the money so to speak."

"That's amazing. Beautiful, smart, and talented," he croons and gives me a smile.

His smile lights up his entire face. His eyes sparkle with the gesture. I look away and glance around for Kordell.

The waitress has already brought our drinks and taken our food orders, but Kordell isn't anywhere in sight. I turn my gaze back to Hershel. I had a few drinks while waiting for Kordell to arrive, but I'm still not in the mood for the bullshit.

"What exactly is going on here? What happened to your friend? I'm supposed to be here for a dinner meeting for some personal business with him but I'm sitting here with you," I say in frustration.

"I'm sure he's still in the restroom."

"Let me ask you one more question."

"Gone on, I'm an open book."

"You and Kordell are best friends you say, right?"

"Yeah, we are."

"It seems you two do everything together. Is that also true?"

"Many things. Yes."

I nod and lock eyes with him. "What does Meet and Breed mean to you?"

I narrow my eyes at him. He drops his head and stares down into his lap. Just as I thought.

I sigh and run a hand through my hair as I try to reel my temper in. I've been patient with these two but that stops here.

"This is important to me. You and your friend are playing games. I don't have time for this.

"Clearly, he's not the one for this. You two assholes can go fuck each other. Stay the hell away from me, Hershel. If you see me, walk the other way. Are we clear?"

"JC, wait. You have it all wrong."

On the verge of tears, I get up and gather my things. All I want is a baby. I don't deserve this.

Everything is falling apart and these two are taking away my chance at the one thing I want desperately. Un-fucking-believable.

"Jodie Cadence?"

I freeze. This night couldn't get any worse. Why me? What have I done to deserve this?

I turn to find guess who staring back at me? None other than my ex, David and his fiancée. I mean, damn, I could have spit this chick out.

She has my hair cut, she's about my height and almost as curvy as I am. The only difference is I know for a fact she's younger than me. In her early twenties while I just turned thirty this year.

"You look nice. Who's this?" David says as he looks Hershel over.

Oh, hell nah. I might be pissed at Hershel and want to kick his ass but he's my mom's boyfriend's son. That makes him ours with his weird ass. When you belong to a Marks, we don't play that shit.

There is also the fact that I don't want David to know what's really going on here. That I've fallen so low to get the baby he promised me. I step into Hershel's side.

"This is my boyfriend," I say as I wrap my arm around Hershel's waist.

Hersh doesn't miss a beat. I'll give him that. He wraps his arm around me and pulls me into his side as he holds his other hand out for David's.

"Hershel Harrington."

"Babe, you're always trying to be so modest. This is Dr. Hershel Harrington. Hersh, this is my ex, David Jones."

I keep to myself that I found out after we broke up that Jones isn't even his real last name. Like I said. So many red flags.

I take pride in who I am. Trying to hide my heritage is a big no for me. I wish I would have known this about him from the beginning.

His being Nigerian wouldn't have stopped me from dating him. However, knowing how much he lies would have. Full stop.

I want to cackle with glee at the sour look that comes to David's face. Little Miss Thing is a micro influencer and drives Uber eats on the side. I guarantee David is missing my six-figure contribution to his life.

He used to purchase a new tailored suit once a week. Before I took off for my vacation from work, I notice he wasn't showing up looking as sharp as he used to.

I'm not knocking the way anyone makes a living, but I know what that table looks like and what I brought to it. David never expected me to find out about them when I did. His ass planned on using me until he was comfortable enough to walk away.

His substitute wasn't coughing up bread like he wanted. Little did he know it wasn't because she didn't want to. She didn't have it to.

Research is a big part of my job. Give me a frappe and a few minutes and I'll have anyone's life story. David should have taken a page from my book before he fucked up the best thing he ever had.

Once I lost all trust in him, I took the blinders off and dove in. When I came up for air, I was covered in lies and shit. Like I said, I'm over him.

"Oh, you're his ex?" This chick says while looking me over then blinking a few times.

I guess she's noticing what I did. She's only a broke version of me. Sounds mean but fuck it. It's the truth.

"Jodie, I know you fucking lying. You're not dating this dude," David laughs.

"Wow, what makes you fix your face to say that?"

"I mean, look at him. Not to mention, I know you. White boys ain't it for you." He lowers his voice to say the last part.

I clench my jaw. In truth, I've never thought to date outside my race. However, I'm not about to let on that he's right.

"You don't know anything about me."

"Okay. Listen, buddy, how long have you two been dating?" David says to Hershel.

"It's been about four months."

"Right, where does she work and what's her title?"

"She works at Caring Hearts and she's the executive director of marketing and social media management," Hershel says with ease.

"Cool. All first date shit. I still don't believe you two have been dating. This smells more like a blind date gone wrong."

"Just because you don't believe it, doesn't change the facts," Hershel says sounding pissed off.

His hold on my waist has tightened and he's pulled me in closer. I have to admit, being this close, his cologne is making my knees weak. He smells delicious.

David gives a sly smile. "If you're dating her, prove it."

"Have you lost your mind?" I hiss.

"Not at all. If he's fucking you this should be easy. What's her favorite food?"

"Chinese food. Egg rolls specifically."

I smile not expecting Hershel to know that or to be so specific. He has spent a lot of time around us since we've been coming to stay at Mom's new house.

"And how does that prove he's fucking me, you jerk?"

"It doesn't, I'm getting there. I just wanted to warm him up."

I scoff. "Oh please. Wait." Hold my hand up. "What are you even doing here?"

"Didn't Gretta tell you. I was sent to help you with the Spring Valley project. I'm not staying on some ranch at some B&B. The nearest five star hotel is here in this town.

"The guy at the hotel we're staying at mentioned the restaurants and bars here, so we came over to get a bite. I'll be working with you on the project from now on. It was Mr. Copeland's idea."

It would be our boss's idea because Gretta knows I don't want to be within ten feet of this man. No wonder she kept changing subjects when I would ask who they were sending.

"Oh, yay me," I bite out bitterly.

"You ready to go?" Hershel asks.

"What's her favorite position?" David deadpans with a shit eating grin.

I turn to Hershel, lift on my toes and pull his head down to mine. He takes over the kiss immediately. Damn, what was my plan?

Hershel groans into my mouth and glides his hand down to my ass. Instantly, I remember what I planned to do—game night we've done this before. I break the kiss as I look up into his eyes and slip my hand beneath the back of his shirt.

I then begin to write the answer against his skin with my fingertip like the game from game night. His eyes fill with lust as he looks back at me. Not looking away from me, he answers David with a smug grin on his lips.

"Not that we have anything to prove to you but as her man, any position I put her in is her favorite when I'm inside her, but doggie style drives her crazy."

I smile up at him then lift on my toes to peck his lips. He places his hand behind my head and deepens the kiss. He's getting carried away with this, but I'm not complaining one bit at the moment.

"Why does any of this matter to you? Hello, did you forget you're here with your fiancée?" Little Miss Thing whines.

I pull away from Hershel, gather my roses and the rest of my things and turn to storm out. Making sure my ass and hips sway on my way. I get outside and about two blocks away before I start to laugh like a mad woman as tears stream down my face.

"JC, JC," Hershel's voice breaks through my mania.

"What?" I scream as I spin on him.

"Why do you hate me so much?"

"I didn't hate you before."

"But you do now?" he says as if he's confused.

"Thanks for the save. Just leave this alone. Okay?"

"No, it's not okay. You felt that. There's something here."

"There is nothing here. What should have been here tonight you blew up in my face. You robbed me for the only option I had. Why do I hate you? Why?"

I crowd his space as I hiss at him. "I hate you because I needed to find a match. I needed Kordell to get the one thing I want, and you royally fucked up the trust I have in that system, so I'm left with nothing, and time is running out.

"I hate you because you're no different from that asshole back there. You robbed me. You selfish motherfuckers keep robbing me."

Tears are running down my face, and my chest is heaving. He cups my face between his palms and licks his lips. Then he searches my gaze with his eyes.

"If you want a baby, I can give you one. You were right, I am on the app. Match with me. Go into an agreement with me.

"Not a stranger. I check all the same boxes as Kordell. Let me be the one," he says before crushing his lips to mine.

CHAPTER THREE

Change of Heart

Jodie Cadence

The other night was a mistake. I mean, the sex was good. Scratch that, the sex was amazing and the conversation after and in between was pleasant.

However, it was a drunken and emotional decision I never should have made. I have a ton of unanswered questions now. That should have been answered before taking Hershel back to my place and allowing him to reconstruct my guts and my common sense.

Questions like how did he know what I'd gone to meet with Kordell about? Why was he there? What the hell were they planning by showing up together?

I stop in the opening of the hallway and watch as Hershel, Jo, Mel, Cash, and Chance all talk excitedly in the living room. This is the biggest reason we shouldn't have gone there. I can hear Jack and Mom in the kitchen.

This is becoming our home. These men are becoming apart of our family whether we want it or not. They look out for us as much as we look out for them.

I haven't even told Mom or my sisters what I'm going through. How am I to have a baby with Hershel and pretend it isn't his? The purpose of the site was to find a donor to sleep with, get my baby and move on.

First, with dick like that, who wants to move on? Second, this will hurt so many people I care about. That was never my intention. Hershel looks up and his eyes light up at the sight of me.

"Fuck me," I huff and turn to head in the other direction for the backyard.

I flop into one of the chairs once back there and run a hand through the front of my bob. This is not what I wanted.

This has become so complicated. I nearly threw up when I walked into the headquarters space, I rented for my team to work out of here in Spring Valley. David stood there looking like he runs the place, barking orders and trying to take over.

"Want to talk about why you've been avoiding me?"

I look up and frown. I didn't hear him follow me. To be honest, I thought everyone would get the point that I want to be alone. My sisters get it.

Everyone knows when I just need to have some space. However, this man doesn't know me. I guess he doesn't know how to read the room either.

"No. I want to talk about how we're going to forget about the other night. It never happened and we can forget about anything we agreed to."

"Why? What's going on?"

"Oh my God. Seriously? I didn't match with you. You weren't my choice.

"I got caught up and did something I shouldn't have. Something that could alter everything and all my views. How don't you get that?"

"Is this because I'm white?"

"Ding, ding, ding," I say widening my eyes at him. "This wasn't shopping for a pair of shoes for me. You can't just swap out one pair for another.

"Kordell is chocolate brown. He would have given me gorgeous coco brown babies with that gorgeous smile. He's tall and athletic. Not to mention smart. There was a reason I chose him."

"I'm at least an inch and a half taller than him. Kordell and I usually tie for top grades, or I'd edge him out by a few points. I was captain of the basketball team and our football squad.

"I'm not ugly, JC. I might not check off the melanin box, but our baby would still be handsome or beautiful like their mother. I'm not saying that you should just swap us out but I'm not a terrible option," he says and frowns.

"Boy, don't make me go upside your head. A. you probably get extra points for things that your professors made up because they can't allow a Black man to best you.

"B. Were you deserving of being captain or did your privilege afford you that one too? Let me explain something to you. I had to do twice the work my counterparts had to because I'm a Black woman.

"I've been overqualified and the most capable in the room and still passed over more times than I can count. You're usually the type who gets what I've worked the hardest for.

"The privileged, clean cut, handsome, rich guy, who walked in knowing he's not as good as me but will still get whatever he wants. Forgive me if all this just rubs me the wrong way," I snap and roll my eyes.

"You don't know me, so you don't know how hard I've worked or how often I've watched that scenario play out in my best friend's life."

"Exactly, you have watched. You have not experienced. Just like I've never experienced being white.

"With all the things I will have to teach my young Black child, you're asking me to give them a biological father who won't be there to answer the things I don't know. Nor will I have the means to buy their way into experiences. I'm well off, but not that well off. Not enough to comfortably say I can pay their way if they don't look the part.

"That's not what I want for my child. I don't want to knowingly make things harder for them. Do you understand?"

He sighs as his gaze searches mine. "I'll be honest. When I saw your profile on Kordell's laptop, I was jealous and wanted it to be me.

"Something about you caught my eye from the first time we met. Kordell and I truly are alike, but I see where my privileged way of thinking has gotten in the way. I'm truly sorry.

"But … can you truly say there isn't something between us? That night was amazing. I'd love it if we could go on a date."

"That would probably be cool if things were different, but I'm still on a clock. I need to see if I can get over what you and Kordell tried to pull so I can find a match. If not, I need to focus on my plan B."

"Do you mind me asking where this clock is coming from? You're thirty, right? You still have time."

"No, Hershel, I don't. I was diagnosed with a rare condition and if I don't conceive in the next two or three years, I could lose my window ever to," I say into my lap.

Hershel stands and comes to squat in front of me. He cups my face, causing me to look up at him. His blue gaze is filled with concern and sympathy.

"Oh, baby, I'm so sorry. I didn't know. I … fuck, I feel like shit.

"Is there anything I can do? I mean, if there is anything you need, I want to help. Damn it, I really do come off as entitled now.

"I'm so fucking sorry. I'm here for whatever you need. If you want to talk or if you need … fuck, I don't know. I'm here," he says gentle as guilt takes over his expression.

"Thanks. For now, can you keep all this to yourself. I haven't told anyone."

"You got it. If … if … you are pregnant from the other night. I just want you to know I'm here."

I nod, not having anything else to say. If I'm honest with myself. It sort of feels good to have a person in all of this.

CHAPTER FOUR

Way Forward

Jodie Cadence

"Jodie, Jodie Cadence," David barks pulling me from my thoughts.

I'm not going to lie. I've had sex with Hershel on the brain for the last few days. I need to keep my ass away from that ranch. Seeing him ride around on horseback shirtless isn't helping my cause.

My cycle came, so there's no baby. I didn't expect to be so bummed about that. I spent an hour in the bathroom crying as the reality set in.

I've been avoiding Hershel even more since. He's sent flowers to my apartment and left DMs on the app. I don't know how to feel about that.

I'm starting to see him as less weird and more so attentive and assessing. He might be a little goofy by my standards, but it's become endearing. I truly think he's a nice guy.

Just not my guy. I want someone who understands my life. Someone to love me and want to do this life thing with me.

I want someone who wants to stay because I mean something to them. However, this isn't the time for that. I need to have a baby. Dating has taken a back seat for now.

"Jodie, jeez, where are you?"

I blink at David a few times as I come out of my thoughts. Just like him to ruin a good moment. I roll my eyes, wanting to throw something at him.

"How can I help you?"

"I need to swap assignments with you. The interviews for the interns at Children's House are today. Something personal has come up.

"I can handle your remote tasks for you, but I'll need you to head over to the house and meet with the candidates. I'm sorry to spring this on you," he says.

No, he's not and he knows damn well I'm not about to hand my work over to him to fuck up. Let alone give him access to the donor list and all my personal contacts. He must think I'm stupid.

Then again, he knows me, so this is just his lazy ass way of getting out of doing anything and getting me to take up the slack. Typical.

"Whatever, I'll handle it."

"I mean, we're raising money for the place, how did this become one of our tasks?" he snorts.

I roll my eyes. "Because it costs to have staff. Staff we haven't raised enough money for.

"Those babies still need to be cared for whether there's money or not, so I made it my business to make sure they're covered until we do get them the money," I snarl.

"You're always going above and beyond. You know that's one of the things I love about you."

"Oh, bless your heart. You think I care about anything you're saying, don't you?"

I want to burst into laughter as he stands with his lips flapping. I've been over his charm. I don't have it in me to hold back how I feel.

David hasn't seen how sarcastic, petty, and cutthroat I can be. I have a mean girl streak a mile long and I've spared him that part of my personality for the most part. Not anymore.

"You know we don't have to be this way to each other. We make a good team when we work together."

"You mean, I make you look good when we work together. Good luck with that. You're going to have to find some other way to stick around after this project. I won't be here for you to leach off. Didn't you say you had somewhere to be?"

"Yeah, I do. We're not done talking."

"Sure, we're not." I wave him off.

I grab my purse and my tablet and head out to my car. I'll have to grab lunch on the way. I laugh to myself as I realize David has always been an entitled asshole.

He doesn't do shit at work but keeps elevating. All that ass kissing does wonders for him. That smile and face don't hurt any. Pretty privilege much.

I'm sick of men who think they're entitled to the world. It's childish and reads immature all day. No real accountability for life at all.

Just a gimme, gimme, gimme mentality. I dodged a bullet with that one. However, I wish I caught it sooner.

"We can only do better from here, sis," I mutter to myself.

Hershel

I really want to get this internship. When I found out about this alternative for my residency, I was all over it. It's a position that's being sponsored by my original residency as they didn't have enough hours to spread between us all with budget cuts.

It will only be for three days out of every week, but it's in Spring Valley. That will allow me time to help on the ranch and at the Vet practice. I try to do as much as I can in the community.

It's how Mom and Pop raised me. I stay busy working and doing my part. I think this internship is going to fit nicely into my life.

"I'm heading out, Mrs. Berk. That fence shouldn't give you any more trouble."

"Oh, Hershel. Thank you so much. Your mama would be so proud of you. I don't know what I would do around here without you. You're a lifesaver," she sings.

I've been stopping by to check on her for the last year since her husband passed on not too long after Mama died. They didn't have children so she's out here on her own and she doesn't want to leave their home.

I remember her and Mama being friends while I was a little boy. She's always been kind. I couldn't imagine not coming by to look after her.

"It's my pleasure, ma'am."

"You want to come in for some lemonade?"

"No, ma'am. Not today. I have an interview I need to get to. I should head home and shower."

"Interview? Are you leaving Paws?"

"No, not yet, ma'am. However, I'm looking to make a few changes in my future."

"Oh, don't let me keep you. Thank you again."

"Later, ma'am. Just give me a ring if anything else needs fixing."

"Will do. Good luck with your interview. I hope you get whatever it is."

"Thanks."

I hop in my truck and see I still have about an hour and a half to get ready and make it to town to the Children's House. I'm excited.

I'm aiming for the on-site medical assistant director position. My advisor put in a glowing recommendation. Kordell is undecided about applying.

He's been talking about going to the city to expand his opportunities. I get it. Like me, Kordell loves a challenge. Now that I've been trying to see things through his lens, I realize things in Kelly and Spring Valley can seem like low hanging fruit.

My best friend isn't one to take something because it's been made easy for him no matter what. I guess that's why it didn't sink in when he and JC tried to show me what I hadn't taken into consideration.

I've never shied away from hard work, but I do realize many things may have come easier to me. After recent talks with Kordell, I get his latest position. He feels his wealth and familiarity will speak for him locally.

If not for my family and the ranch, I think I would agree with leaving. I could never know what it's like to be in JC or Kordell's shoes, but I'm trying to be more understanding. That's why I've been giving JC her space.

I would love to date her, and I do wish we could have continued the agreement until she got her baby, but that's what I want. I've realized how much what she wants means to me.

"Can you come help with these barrels?" Chance asks as I head for the door after my shower.

I look at my watch and sigh. "Not right now. I have an appointment to get to."

"Don't worry about it. I'll get it done. You look nice. You going on a date or something?"

"Not a date. Listen, we'll talk later."

He nods and heads for the back to head to the brewery. I make a beeline for the front door before anyone else can stop me. My mind goes to how some day I'll be able to practice human medicine right here in Spring Valley.

"You've got this, Hersh."

Jodie Cadence

"I liked her, but she doesn't seem too comfortable around multiple children at once. She seemed overwhelmed once there was more than one in her care," Dr. Norick, the executive medical director says.

"You noticed that too?"

"I did. I was hoping we'd find someone willing to jump in if we're short staffed, which happens often."

"Well, I believe we have two more."

She flips her hair and turns the pages on her clipboard. I like Sandy, she's been cool anytime I've run into her whether in town or here at the Children's House.

"Yes, there are three more candidates. Mr. Miller, Mr. Harrington, and Miss Desoto."

"Okay, who's next?"

"Mr. Harrington. Ah, here he is."

I look up and lock eyes with none other than Hershel. I want to palm my forehead. Why didn't the name ring a bell?

If it had, I would have found an excuse to avoid this one. Instead, I'll now be stuck with this man for the next hour as if I haven't been daydreaming about him all morning. Fuck me.

CHAPTER FIVE

A Different View

Jodie Cadence

Two weeks later …

I stand leaning up against the wall with my arms folded across my chest as I watch Hershel with a few of the kids. Dr. Norick thought he was perfect.

I'll admit, watching him interact that day with the children was heartwarming. I think I may have judged Hershel a bit harshly from the beginning.

He's not weird at all. He's actually very intelligent, caring, and thoughtful. Now that he's not always trying to talk my ear off to impress me, I've seen him in a different light.

"He's a gorgeous man, isn't he?" Sandy says as she comes to my side.

I shrug. "He's handsome. I'll give him that."

"Don't tell my fiancé but I would totally date him if I were single," she snickers.

"Why, Dr. Norick, are you saying that you're crushing on our new assistant director. Isn't that against your contract?"

"Jodie Cadence, that man isn't worried about me and I'm not his type anyway," she snorts.

"What makes you say that?"

"I've seen the way he looks at you. I do believe he has the hots for you. Maybe the hots is the wrong way to put it. He looks at you like a man falling in love."

"Nope, you're not seeing that at all."

"If you say so. I don't really like David for you. Now the way he looks at you is something totally different. He makes me feel like I need to protect you."

"Don't worry. No one cares about David or what he's on."

"Ugh, speaking of the devil."

I look to see David storming his way in my direction. As I look him over, I want to burst into laughter. His suit is covered in what looks like someone's return of their lunch as he holds his arms out with a scowl on his face.

"Do those kids have any idea how much this suit costs? He just puked all over me. Why are we even here?

"I thought the goal was to help the town gain interest and funnel money into it. What does that have to do with this orphanage? If I had known this ..."

He cuts off as he looks at me glaring at him. One thing has been very clear since David has arrived in town. He sucks with children. They don't even like him.

"This orphanage is special. The children here are all talented and display high potential in the arts. A few years ago, it was the source of high interest.

"Collectors came to buy art. Families came to adopt. Spring Valley had a ton of traffic all because of Children's House alone.

"With what we do at Caring Hearts, I know we can revitalize its presence and impact on both the community and in these children's lives," I bite out.

"Well, I need to change. I'm taking my break. We can brainstorm some more when I return."

I roll my eyes. This is just an excuse for him to get out of here. It's not like he was trying to help anyway.

"Miss Jodie, Miss Jodie." Ariel, one of the cutest little girls ever sings as she comes running over to me. "Dr. Harrington said we can go horseback riding at his ranch for a field trip. I want to paint the horses after. This is so exciting."

Ariel is an exceptional painter. She's so talented for a six-year-old. I was in awe the first time I saw some of her work.

"Oh wow, that is exciting."

I look up at Hershel as he comes over. He's blushing and looking like a kid with his hand in the cookie jar.

"Ariel, why don't you come with me," Dr. Norick says as she holds her hand out.

They walk off and I tilt my head at Hershel. He reaches to rub he back of his neck. I can't help but smile at him.

"Should you be promising them shit like that?" David snares.

"Should you be using language like that?" Hersh tosses back.

"None of them are around. Thank God."

"Wow," I scoff.

"I'll cover the expense. We used to do things like this all the time. I didn't mean to cause a problem.

"I mentioned the horses and said maybe someday there could be the opportunity. Ariel ran with it from there."

"Sounds like her." I laugh. "Don't worry about it. We'll make it happen. It will be fun."

"If this had been my suggestion, you would have bit my head off. Your little boyfriend screws up and it's all good?" David says while narrowing his eyes at me.

"Shouldn't you go clean up? You don't want that to stain."

He snorts and storms off. I shake my head and pull a face. What did I ever see in him?

"Listen, I really didn't mean for that to happen. They're all so cute and when you get to talking to them, you forget—"

"It's fine, Hersh. Like I said, I'll take care of it. You're really good with them. That's the most I've seen Ariel smile since I met her.

"Well, that's good. I'm happy I could help. I'm really loving it here. The staff, the kids, everyone here is great. My hours at the clinic aren't nearly as enjoyable."

"We're happy to have you."

"Are you sure? This hasn't been an inconvenience to you, has it?"

"I'm a big girl. I know how to separate work from my personal life."

"That makes one person."

"What do you mean by that?"

"Your ex is an a-hole," he drops his voice to say. "He's cornered me a few times to ask personal questions about us."

"Like what?" I say as I stand with my mouth open.

"Like what that little tat is on your inner thigh and whether you wax or shave. He's a tool."

"You can say that again. Wow, Hersh, I'm so sorry I dragged you into this."

He gives me a smile. "That's the second time you've called me that. It's not a problem. I wanted to be dragged deeper into things. However, that wasn't in the cards."

"Doesn't mean we can't be friends, right?"

"Right."

"Jodie Cadence, Jodie," Dr. Norick comes rushing over in a panic.

"What is it?"

"No one for the night shift has clocked in. I called them all to find out what's going on. Sarah says she has the flu. Billy said his car broke down and Albert didn't bother to answer my call.

"This has never happened. I don't even know what to do. You're the acting director for now, so … do you need me to stay? I can call Rob and tell him not to pick me up."

"No, you go on home. I'll stay."

"I can stay with you. It's no problem. I didn't have any plans," Hershel offers.

"Are you sure?" Sandy and I ask in unison.

"Sure, why not. I promised the boys we'd play some board games." He looks down at his watch. "Now we'll have plenty of time."

"That's great. I didn't want to leave you all on your own," Dr. Norick says to me. "I saw David rush out not too long ago."

"Like he would have stayed," Hershel and I mutter at the same time.

We look at each other and smile. Yeah, Hershel isn't so bad. This is the second time he's come through for me.

I'm counting the fact that he hasn't told Mom and my sisters my secret. The more I get to know him, the cooler he gets. *Thank you*, I mouth.

No problem, he mouths back and winks. Yup, he's damn handsome too. Ugh, this is not the time to flashback to that night. Not. Right. Now.

David

I want this project to be over. Jodie Cadence is better than this. There are bigger fish to fry in the city.

I want to go home, and I want to go home now. There is no real money in doing this project. I need to be where the real donors and opportunities are.

If I have to pay a couple of people to make that happen, so be it. If it gets back to Caring Hearts that this project is a bust, they will pull out. That's why I called the night staff and paid them all not to show up. However, now as I watch Dr. Norick leave and Jodie Cadence and that asshole are still inside, I see where I fucked up.

"Shit, this isn't supposed to be happening," I yell into my car.

JC was never supposed to find out about Danielle. Danielle was for fun. Being an influencer and traveling all over had its potential. I had been working out my angle to make it all work for me.

However, she lied about how much money she was making as an influencer, and I thought she was living a lifestyle that wasn't real. I only found all of that out after I lost JC. It was Jodie Cadence's words that made me dig deeper. Now I see it was all a fucking mistake.

I proposed to get Danielle to shut the fuck up. To this day I think she's the one who made sure Jodie Cadence found out about her.

"Fucking bullshit. That's what all of this is."

Now this asshole is sniffing around my woman. I still don't think they're dating but he wants her. I'm going to put an end to that shit if it's the last thing I do.

Hershel

I look up and find JC watching me as I finish helping Corey with his pajamas. He's one of the shy kids around here. Talented pianist but not much for making friends on his own.

Knowing what that's like, I've tried to help him with that. If not for my mama's encouragement, I don't think I would have had as many friends growing up. I'm still not the most outgoing guy.

"You all set?" I say to Corey.

"Yeah, thanks. Goodnight, Dr. Harrington."

"Goodnight, buddy."

He gives me a warm smile and then as if a last-minute thought, he throws his arms around my neck. I embrace him and give him a tight squeeze.

I'm falling in love with this assignment more and more each day. I really feel like I'm making a difference. I stand from his bed and allow him to climb in, then tuck him in.

Once he's all set, I go to check on the others. Finding half the little guys fast asleep and the other half on their way, I turn to leave out of the room.

"That was sweet of you. I think Corey likes you," JC says as we begin to walk the hallway together.

"He's a good kid. Shy but smart and sweet."

"That he is. Do you find that's why you connect with him? Because he's shy."

I shrug. "That has a lot to do with it, I guess."

"I think you're going to make a wonderful pediatrician. Have you decided when you're going to tell your family?"

"No, not yet. I don't know what's holding me back. Mom knew. She's the one who encouraged me to see it through. I think not telling Pop or Chance has a lot to do with having that one last thing that was special between us."

"That makes sense."

"So what should we do now? Want to head to the game room?"

"You don't have paperwork you need to get to? They kept you busy all day."

"Nope, I'm all caught up. I can get the Connect Four set up. We can finally settle all the trash talk."

"You're a glutton for punishment, I see."

"If you say so."

We make our way to the game room and settle in. Once again, I look up to find her watching me closely. I place my elbow on the table and rest my cheek on my fist.

"What?"

"Nothing," she breathes and shakes her head.

The breathy sound of her voice throws me back to that night. I can't help dropping my gaze to her lips. I remember the passion in her voice as we made love.

"Hershel, oh God, yes," she cried out as I went down on her after we got to her place.

We barely made it through the door before I helped her peel her dress off and tossed it to the floor. Holding her gaze, I dropped to my knees and peeled her panties down her legs. I then hooked her leg over my shoulder and dove in to feast on her.

She smelled and tasted amazing. I couldn't help but run my hands all over her soft curves while eating her pussy like it was my last meal. My mouth watered as I pulled back and looked at her fat mound.

I pushed my fingers into her as I climbed back to my feet and took her lips. She rode my fingers as I devoured her mouth. Not breaking the kiss, she reached for my shirt and started on the buttons.

I groaned into her mouth as she pushed my shirt from my shoulders. I only pulled my hand from her core long enough to let my shirt fall to the floor. I break the seal of our lips to breath her in as the sound of her juices filled the air around us. She was so wet.

"Hershel," she moaned as I moved my lips to her neck and sucked the skin there into my mouth.

Palming her breast with my free hand, I then kissed my way to her nipple and captured it into my mouth. She bucked her back away from the door I had her pressed against and cried out.

I kept fingering her tight core as I sucked on her peek. JC pulled my belt from my pants and unfastened them. As my belt clattered to the floor, she pushed my pants down my hips.

"Yes, right there. Oh shit, Hershel. Yes, yes," she cried.

Soon her body started to tremble, and she came all over my hand. With a satisfied grin on my lips, I pulled my fingers from her body and lifted them to my mouth.

"Mm," I hummed around my fingers as I sucked them clean.

"Come with me," she said as she looked up at me while linking our fingers together.

"Hershel, are you okay?"

"Um?"

"You zoned out. Are you all right?"

"Oh, yeah. I was thinking."

"Mind if I ask what about?"

"Maybe some other time."

"Do you regret that night?" She asks tilting her head to the side.

"What? Are you serious?"

"Yeah, I want to know if you have any regrets."

"Actually, I do. I regret how I went about things. I wish I knew more about how you felt and why you were on that app to begin with.

"Selfishly, I would still want it to be me. However, I wouldn't have ruined your experience. I wish I could erase how I made you feel so you could find someone to have your baby with."

"Is that all you regret?"

"No, I regret that things didn't continue the way I thought they would have. I regret that I haven't gotten a call from you saying we did it, we made a baby."

"We didn't. My cycle came. I was disappointed but I've been working that out so I can decide what's next."

"Disappointed? Really?"

"Yes, Hershel. I don't like to fail, and I really want a baby."

"What are your options now? If you don't mind me asking."

"I don't know. I deleted the app. That's a no for me."

I chuckle. "Yeah, I know what you mean. I deleted my profile too."

She tilts her head to the other side and studies me. "What were you doing on there to begin with? Do you truly want to have a baby with some random?"

"No, not at all. Kordell told me about the site. I thought he was crazy.

"I had to turn in a work study assignment and needed to use his laptop. That's when I saw your profile and that you two had matched.

"I only signed up to go through the process because like I said, I wanted to be your person. I thought if you got to know me away from Spring Valley, away from our families then maybe you would see me.

"I've been shy all my life. Sometimes I can't put myself out there like everyone else. You didn't give me a chance to.

"I felt like you judged me before I got to show you who I am. I just screwed everything up after signing up," I try to explain.

"So you only joined because of me? Is that what you're saying?"

"Yeah, I don't know if you know this, but you're sort of amazing. Beautiful, smart, talented, and God, woman, you can cook. I think you'll make an amazing mother.

"I wanted to be your person and help you to do that. It didn't feel right for it to be anyone else. Not when it could be me," I answer.

JC laughs. "Shy, but you don't lack confidence. That's for sure."

"Never have," I say with a smile.

"Okay, Hersh. I see you. Not that you shouldn't be confident."

I don't miss the smirk on her lips as she looks back at me with mirth dancing in her eyes. I could sit here staring at her all night. Whoever gets to be the man in her life is one lucky bastard, that's for sure.

"Tell me more about what makes you tick, Dr. Harrington. We have all night," she says as she drops a checker into a slot.

"Not much to tell." I shrug and take my turn. "What do you want to know?"

She sits thinking for a moment while making the cutest face. I can't help thinking that she's letting her guard down. This is the most open she's been around me since that night we spent together.

"If you could change anything in your life, what would it be?" she says after a beat.

"I used to hate living on the ranch. We had to get up early to help out. Stepping in cow and horse shit in the morning never went over well in school."

"Oh no."

I chuckle. "I think the only reason I was popular in high school is because I could supply the beer."

She laughs and it lights up her face. "I bet."

"I didn't mind. I liked being the one to help out. I've always been the guy everyone could call to help."

"I know what you mean. I don't jump up to help just anyone, but I do help those in need. I'm big on the underdog."

"I can see that. With your job and all. That truly makes sense."

"I'm sure life was way more interesting in the city."

She shrugs. "Everything is about perception. I'm sure you would feel differently if we traded places."

"Maybe. Sometimes you just need to take a chance on where you are and see if that's what fits."

"Mm," she hums.

CHAPTER SIX

Breakfast On Me

Jodie Candence

"Your stomach sounds like it's going to eat you if you don't feed it. Let me treat you to breakfast," Hershel says as we step out of Children's House and head for our cars.

I have to be honest, I am hungry, but I'm just as tired. I could fall flat on my face and sleep for a week. There's no way I'm heading to my apartment.

I plan to go to Mom's and crash there. After all, I had planned to stay with Mom anyway while she recovers. Jo needs to head back to the city for work.

She's been taking care of Mom for the last two weeks. We were all so scared after Mom's accident. I know I've been thinking about my life a lot more after.

"Sure, why not," I say to Hershel.

I've enjoyed our time together and I'm not sure I'm ready to part ways. He's more interesting than I thought. He kept me up laughing most of the night.

"Shelby's sound good?"

"Yes, that would be perfect. It's right up the street. I don't think I could make the drive anywhere else."

"I'd be happy to drive you home. I could get your car to you later."

"I'll be fine. Thanks though."

"Anytime."

He places a hand on the small of my back and leads me toward Shelby's. Warmth spreads through me from the simple touch. Once again, my thoughts try to float back to that night.

Hershel knows what he's doing in the bedroom. He did not disappoint in that department. I felt him for days after.

"Are you cold? Would you like my jacket?" he asks as a shiver that has nothing to do with the weather runs through me.

"No. I'm fine. Thanks."

I realize he quickens his step a bit. I smile knowing he's doing it to get me out of the cool morning air. He even tugs me a little closer to his body heat.

We make it to Shelby's and Alice is there waiting with a big smile on her face. I inhale deeply, allowing the scent of the coffee and freshly baked goods to fill my lungs.

"Good morning, you two," Alice says.

"Good, morning, Alice," we say in unison.

"What can I get for you? I have some muffins that are fresh out of the oven. I have some Blueberry and some Orange-cranberry. Or can I get you something else?"

"I'll take the Orange-cranberry muffin and some of the salted caramel coffee."

"And let me guess, your usual," she says to Hershel.

"No, ma'am. I want to try what she's having."

"Coming right up."

We move to a booth and have a seat. Placing my elbow on the table, I then lean my head on my palm and close my eyes. I want to fire the night shift, but it's going to be hard to replace them.

For now, they're going to get lucky. I'm going to write all their asses up though. It's the no call, no show for me.

"Thank you," Hershel says.

"It's good to see you, Hershel. I've missed our late-night dates."

I open my eyes and lift a brow at him. I smile in amusement as his cheeks pink slightly. He gives Alice a charming smile.

"I've missed our visits too."

"You're such a sweet boy. Did you know he used to bring his books in and would sit with me as I baked late at night?"

"No, I didn't know that."

"All the ladies in town chirp about this one being one of the good ones. I'm surprised some young lady hasn't snagged him up already," she goes on. "Well, let me get out of your hair. I have some cookies I want to get in the oven."

"You would come in and study here, didn't you?" I say once Alice is out of ear shot.

"She thought I was bookkeeping for Pop but yeah. She keeps such late hours. It didn't sit well with me that she would leave here all times of the night on her own. It was the least I could do.

"I just haven't had the time lately, but I still worry about her. I'll have to stop in soon. I think we both got used to the company," he says.

"That's so sweet. You know she's thinking about selling."

"I heard whispers. I didn't know if any of them were true."

"They are. I'm still tossing around the idea of purchasing the place from her. I would open the main kitchen back up and do more than bake."

"That would be awesome. I'll be your first customer. In fact, if you need someone to test recipes out on, I'm all for it," he says and rubs his stomach.

"I'll keep that in mind."

"What's holding you back?"

"I did a walk through and there are some repairs I would need to address. I would have to leave Caring Hearts and if I have a baby …"

"That would take up your time."

"Yeah, I know Mom would help, but I don't want to put that on her. She's done enough for me and Mel."

"I'm sure she doesn't see it that way."

I shrug and knit my brows. "It's starting to feel selfish to want to do things this way. You know, find a donor who's not going to be there."

"Then why not find someone who wants to be a part of the process and the baby's life?"

"I can barely find a donor dad," I snort.

"Hear me out. Your main concern is not being able to teach a baby with me the things you don't know about being my race. What if you didn't have to teach them any of that because I can? I can be there to help.

"Pop and Coral have been going strong once again. We already have a family willing to support us. I don't want more than to help. You wouldn't owe me anything in return.

"You get your baby, you'll be able to buy this place, and I'll handle the repairs. You can have it all, JC. Time doesn't have to run out. We can start as soon as you're ready," he says sincerely.

"What if things don't work out between us. That will make things awkward for everyone. I don't know."

"That's why I'm doing this for you as a friend. I like you and I would like to have more, but I want this for you above anything else. If that means, I'm in the friend zone, so be it."

"You're serious, aren't you?"

"Yes, I did the physical. Everything checks out. I can give you this if you let me."

I sigh and sit looking down at the table. I have so many things running through my head. Including that clock ticking in the back of my mind.

"I don't want to give my baby false hope. If you're going to be there, I want you to be there. This can't be like my father.

"He broke our hearts. I'm still working through that pain. You have no idea how it feels to be unwanted by the one who made you."

"I'm not him, JC. Anytime our baby needs me, I'll be there. It's not in my nature not to be. I don't know how to abandon the people I love.

"Just think about it. We don't have to tell anyone. It can be our secret until you're ready. Heck, David already thinks we're together."

"Okay, I'll think about it. Can you give me some time to process?"

"Of course. Call me whenever you're ready. I'm here to listen if you want to talk it out as well."

I nod and sip at my coffee. Do I want to have a baby with this man? What other options do I have?

Just the thought of those options causes my chest to tighten as if I'm about to have a panic attack. This might be the path I have to take. The only one I can get through.

Hershel

I would be lying if I said JC isn't still on my mind. It broke my heart when she mentioned her father and how she feels when it comes to him. I got to know so much about her last night and this morning.

I want a real relationship with her, but if this is all we can have, I want to give her this. I want to be a father. The thought of being a father to JC's baby feels right. Hearing her say she was disappointed not to be pregnant by me stirred something in me.

"Hey, you all right over here? Can I get you anything?" Lauren asks as I sit at one of the tables out back where the customers dine.

"I'm fine. Thanks."

"Do you mind if I take a seat? Things have been slow tonight. First night in a long time we haven't been packed wall to wall," she says with a smile.

"Gone on, take a load off. Give it another hour and you can clock out and take off. I just want to make sure we don't get a rush after that concert."

She palms for forehead. "Oh, I forgot about that. There are so many new cool things happening in town. I'm still getting used to the changes."

"Yeah, a lot of good things have been happening."

"I heard a rumor you're working at the Children's House."

"I am."

"Is it true you're a doctor there?"

I sigh. "Yeah. I'm finishing my human residency there. I haven't told Pop or Chance yet, so keep the truth of the rumor to yourself for now, please."

"My lips are sealed. That's so wonderful. I guess you really don't have time to date now," she says.

"I don't have much time for anything right now. However, I make time for what's important to me."

Her eyes light up. "Oh, well, I want to catch one of those concerts in town while they're happening. I was wondering if you—"

My phone rings and JC's name lights the screen. "Hold that thought, I need to take this."

"Oh, okay," she says and her shoulders slump.

"Hello," I say as I get up and answer the call.

"Hey, it's me. I've been thinking about what you said this morning. I did some journaling to work through my feelings and thoughts.

"Would you mind meeting me in Kelly tomorrow at my place so we can talk? I want to hash out the details if we're to go forward with this."

"Yeah, I can be there. What time were you thinking?"

"Around three. Is that good for you?"

"Yeah. Perfect. My morning hours will be done at the clinic by then and I'll be finished on the ranch."

"Okay, see you then. Thanks, Hersh."

"No problem. See you then," I say and hang up.

I turn and head back to the table where Lauren is still sitting. I give her a smile, feeling lighter than I did a few moments ago. JC is giving things some thought.

"You should take a night off and go to the concert. Just let me know which night you're going, and I'll work out the schedule," I say to Lauren and pat her on the shoulder.

I then walk off whistling. Things are looking up. I might be a father this time next year.

CHAPTER SEVEN

Can We Do This

Jodie Cadence

I've thought long and hard about this. Hershel is right about one thing. Things would be different if the father of my child could teach them all the things I can't.

I've got them on the Black experience. However, if I chose a father of another race, it would be important to me that he's a part of their lives to teach them all the things about the other part of themselves.

Then there is the fact that I do want my child to have a father figure in their life. My expiring clock shouldn't take that from him or her. These thoughts are what kept me up all day even though I should have been resting.

After some journaling, when I knew I wouldn't be able to sleep until I followed through with making a choice, I called Hershel. This has been a huge leap for me. I want to control the situation so much but I'm going to have to let go.

"I promise. I'm in this with you, JC. I'm not here to hurt you or our child. If you chose to do this with me, I'm here," Hershel murmurs as he searches my face with his blue eyes as we sit in the living room in my apartment.

"I want to believe you. I'll only do this with you if I know I can trust you. I think you already know trust doesn't come easy with me.

"I'm working on that. I had a band-aide on my trust until David. Now those wounds are old, rotten, and festering. That's not yours to fix or bear, but I will need your patience if we're going to do this," I think out loud.

"You have my patience. You also have me to help. It might not be my burden, but you can lean on me. You don't have to do any of this alone."

"But why?"

I furrow my brows as I look back at him with questioning eyes. I get that he wants to help me. It's in his nature to help as I've come to learn about him. I just want to know why help me and why like this?

"I have this feeling in my gut like if I don't do this we will regret not trying or doing something about this growing connection between us. Tell me you don't feel it, and I'll back off. You feel it too, don't you?

"It may scare you, but you feel it too. I see it when I look in your eyes. Am I wrong?" he says in a soothing tone.

It's almost like he's talking to a scared child. That might have rubbed me the wrong way with someone else, but I'm starting to gravitate toward this man's patience. It's going a long way in telling me he sees me.

I look down into my lap to break the intense connection I feel between us. He cups the side of my cheek and lifts my face with his thumb under my chin. I'm thrown back to that night we spent together and the connection I felt forming as he took my body like he knew it was his.

I realize that I do trust him. That's why he's here now. It's also why I agreed to his hire at Children's House.

He makes me feel safe. He gives me the feeling of something familiar. Hershel makes me feel at home.

"No, you're not wrong. I … I just don't know what this means. I'm asking you for a baby, but I get this feeling like you're asking for something more."

"I'm only asking for you to let me in. Take my friendship. Allow me to help you accomplish this dream.

"No matter what I'm going to be a father to our child. I'm going to be a friend to you and I'll be the support system you desire. Anything on top of that would be a blessing, but you owe me nothing. I'll even be your pretend boyfriend around David to get in his craw."

We both laugh lightly. David has been trying to get on our last nerves, but this isn't about him. He's a nonfactor at this point.

"What if you fall in love with someone during the process? Where does that leave me and the baby?" I chew on my lip as I think this over.

"We can put things in writing if you like. If either of us finds someone else we'll remain in the baby's life, but we'll respect the personal space of the other party. I want to make this as easy as possible for you," he says.

I nod and lick my lips. This is so crazy. How did we get here?

"And if we catch feelings for each other? Shouldn't we have a safe word or something? You know, to let the other one know our feelings are involved. I don't want to hurt you and I'm not trying to be hurt."

He looks away as I watch him swallow hard. I expect this to be the moment he has clarity and calls this all off. However, Hershel keeps surprising me.

"Clouded views," he says.

"Huh?"

"That's my safe word. If I catch feelings, I'll tell you that I have clouded views."

"Okay, cool." I nod and think for a moment. "Folded. If I catch feelings, I tell you that I've folded."

He chuckles. "That sounds like you."

"It's a song I was listening to earlier as I was thinking. It's by Kehlani. She's actually talking about being undecided and sort of fickle.

"She wants space, but she's mad when her partner doesn't come running. She's pushing them away and begging them to stay at the same time. Then she places the ball back in her partner's lap by telling them to come and pick up their clothes she's already folded. It does sound like me."

"Okay so, I'll tell you when my views are clouded and you'll tell me when you have my shit folded. If you find someone you want to be with after we do this, you come to me and let me know. If the shoe is on the other foot, I'll come to you," he says.

"And for now ..."

"We work on making a baby. I can come here to Kelly if you don't want anyone to know about it. We can tell our families when you're ready."

"Hershel?"

"Yes."

"Thank you," I choke out.

He winks at me. "I'm here, darlin'. Let's get you a baby."

Hershel

I cup the back of her neck and press my lips to her forehead. It's an intimate gesture. I know but I'm not able to help myself.

JC stands and holds her hand out to me. "Come with me," she whispers.

I nod and take her offered hand as I stand. She turns and leads me to her bedroom. This feels different from last time.

I don't know if I can say I was nervous the first time we slept together. Not like this. I'm not nervous about the act.

I'm nervous about the outcome. That clock is ticking in the back of my head now, and I don't want to let JC down. I pushed for this, so I need to deliver.

However, first and foremost, I want her to be at ease. As we enter her room and she turns to me, I'm not sure that's the case. Her brown eyes are locked on mine and I see all the things swirling in them.

Wanting this, not wanting this, all the questions and concerns. Her needs that go beyond the physical and tap into the mental and emotional sides of her. There are so many emotions warring on her face.

"Relax. I know what you like. Be in the moment and enjoy," I murmur as I lean in and take her lips.

The moment our lips touch I feel her body relax in my embrace. Our tongues dance together and we deepen the kiss. When she locks her arms around my neck and tugs me closer, I groan into her mouth.

There's no alcohol involved this time. It's me, her, and our shared mission to give her the family she wants. Everything else falls away and I get lost in the moment.

She breaks the kiss and steps back to begin to undress me. I brush her cheek with my fingertips as she releases the buttons on my shirt. Her touch is electric as she sticks her hands into my shirt and runs her palms up my sides.

Once she reaches my shoulders, she pushes the shirt to the floor. I cup the side of her face and run my thumb across her lower lip. She looks up from releasing my belt and locks eyes with me.

A small smile comes to her lips. I press against the soft flesh. JC takes the tip of my thumb into her mouth and bites down on it.

I'm hard as a rock as she pushes my jeans down my hips. Not able to hold back a second longer, I dip my head in and take her lips in a searing kiss. She moans into my mouth as I palm her ass and drag her body into mine.

"Hersh," she breaks the kiss to gasp as I bunch the skirt of her dress up.

"Yeah, baby, what do you need?"

She turns and tilts her head to the side. I smile and lean in to kiss her neck as I reach for the zipper on her dress. With my other hand, I reach around her body and palm her breast over the fabric of her dress.

"You smell so good, baby," I whisper in her ear as I get the fastening all the way down to it's stop.

Hooking my fingers into the neckline of the dress, I push it down the front of her body and allow it to fall to her feet. Her ass comes into view in a pair of lacy boy shorts. My mouth is watering as I take her in.

"Hersh, yes," she breaths as I reach around her body to cup her sex while I plant kisses against her soft back.

I snake my fingers into her panties and shove them into her waiting core. I keep kissing, licking, and sucking at her smooth flesh as I prime her wet pussy for me.

Planting my free palm on her back, I then bend her at the waist as I get to my knees. I'm not going to rush this. There's no reason we shouldn't enjoy this process. In fact, it's better if she does.

I kiss every inch of her like I own this sexy body she's allowing me to please. It's crazy how well we fit together. Hooking my fingers into her panties, I then peel them down and reveal her wet core.

As I kiss each cheek and drag my tongue across her skin, I claw my fingertips up her legs. Goose bumps rise all over her skin as she moans.

Spreading her cheeks, I then dive in and feast on her. My name has never sound sweeter. Each time she calls it, I feel more and more like hers.

I keep devouring her and pulling her pleasure to the surface. As I add my fingers to the feast, she gets louder. I reach to stroke myself becoming impatient to have her.

"Hershel," she cries out as she comes.

With a grin on my lips, I pull back and wipe her juices from my face. I get to my feet and guide her to the side of the bed where I bend her over. I know from experience and her own admission that she loves it doggie style.

"Jodie," I groan as I thrust into her tight heat.

She looks back at me as she bites her lip. I grab her waist and slow down my thrusts. It feels amazing but I don't want this to end too fast.

"Oh shit, Hershel," she cries.

"Fuck, baby. So fucking good."

"Yes, yes, just like that. Make that pussy come."

"Yeah, baby, that's what you want. You want me to come in this wet ass pussy? You want me to coat your walls with my cum?"

"Yes, please. I need you to fill me up. Can you do that for me?"

"Yes, baby. I'm going to do that for you right after I fuck you so good you forget your name."

"Oh fuck, yes," she whimpers as she grabs the sheets and start to throw it back at me. "You're so hard and deep inside me. Yes."

Lifting my leg, I plant my foot on the mattress beside her and really get into it. My eyes roll back, and I throw my head back. I can't help but to close my eyes as I lunge into her core.

"Fuck, Jodie, shit baby."

The sound of her wet pussy is the perfect soundtrack for this amazing sex. She reaches back and tries to hold me off, causing me to open my eyes and drop my head.

I hold off a bit, but she starts to throw it back more. I bite my lip and groan as I watch her ass as I thrust in and out of her. Sweat is dripping down my face and chest.

There is a sheen of sweat beginning to dew on her back as well. I growl deep when I feel her squeeze around my length. All tenderness goes out the window, and I begin to fuck the shit out of her.

She doesn't stop me. Instead, she begs me for more. If we don't make this happen tonight, it's not from a lack of trying.

"Fuck," I roar sometime later as I come deep inside her.

CHAPTER EIGHT

Outside the Bed

Hershel

Two weeks later …

JC looks gorgeous tonight. The patent leather heels, the purple off the shoulder top, and fitted black skirt accent her shape perfectly. I'm six-three.

She and I make a perfect fit. She meets just under my chin. Taller than Mel or Jo, she carries all those lush curves well. I'd be lying if I said I haven't been enjoying my time in her bed.

However, I crave more time in her presence outside of the bedroom. That's why I asked her out tonight. I know this is walking the line, but I couldn't help myself.

"This place is nice. Thanks for inviting me out to dinner," JC says as she looks over the menu.

I brought her out to a restaurant in Kelly close to her apartment. It's a pretty upscale establishment. The kind of place you take a date you want to impress.

"I thought it would be nice to sit down and eat. I know what I come here to do, but I don't want it to feel like that's all I come to Kelly for."

"Well, you do come here for the other part of your residency," she says with a smile.

"You know what I mean."

"Yeah, I do. I was going to invite you over to watch a movie or something. It is kind of weird that you've been to my place to drop your drawers every night for the last two weeks, but we do nothing else."

I chuckle. "We talk. We've been talking a lot."

"This is true, but we should be getting to know each other outside of my bedroom. Our bodies can't be all we know about each other. Besides, this is nice."

I smile and wink at her. "I think we know each other very well when it comes to that."

She bites back a smile. God, I love how her eyes sparkle back at me. The last two weeks have been amazing between us.

The chemistry is off the charts. I'm also getting to know another side of JC. She's been opening up to me more and more.

I'm getting to know the loving, caring, funny JC. In return, I've been my true self. She gets me and all my quirks.

I never have to explain what I mean because she understands how I think, and she anticipates me. If we were dating for real, I'd be falling hard and fast.

"I was thinking. Kelly is nice and all but wouldn't you rather live closer? Like in Spring Valley," I ask.

JC clears her throat and places her drink down. "I've been thinking about that. I have a meeting with Alice about the purchase of Shelby's.

"I think I'm going to move in with Mom for now. We should discuss how we plan to continue meeting up until I'm pregnant. This isn't the way I want her to find out. Meanwhile, I can look for a place in Spring Valley."

"About that. I plan to take care of you guys and all your needs. Chance is building that house for Jo. What would you think about living on WillowBrook lane?

"I could build you guys a place next door to Miss Coral or next to Jo and Chance. Or we could pick a spot further out. You can help me plan it. Make one side of the house for you and the other for me. Make the perfect home for our family."

"Hold on, wait a minute. Since when is Chance building anything for Jo? Does she know about this?"

"Shit," I mutter under my breath and pull a hand down my face.

How the hell did I let that slip? Chance is going to kill me. He didn't want anyone to know that he's building that place for Jo. I shouldn't have opened my big mouth, JC just makes me feel so at ease.

I lick my lips. "No, she doesn't know. Can you please not say anything? I wasn't supposed to tell anyone."

She laughs. "You Harringtons are really something."

"Chance cares about Jo. He's only trying to show her how much. Miss Coral is the one who advised him to show Jo how he feels."

"So he builds her a house?"

"Yeah, he's building her dream home. Meanwhile, he's working on trying to build a relationship with her. After getting to know Jo, I think the two of them fit."

"Better than you and she did?"

"Uh, about that—"

"You're cool. I actually love this for her. I'm only messing with you. Jodie Ann is gorgeous. She carries this light everyone wants to be close to."

"Yeah, she does, but she's not the only one. You light up everything around you. I have a good time whenever I'm around you."

"Enough to live with me? You really want to build a house for us to share?"

"Yes, I would love to live with you and the baby. I can help out with feedings and when it's time to take them to school. We'll be building from scratch so we can make it the perfect place so we're not in each other's hair."

She tilts her head to the side as she smiles at me. That smile is breathtaking. It lights up her face and that bob frames her features perfectly.

"Can I think about it?"

"Yeah, sure. Whenever you're ready. If you don't want to live with me, I'll still build a place for the two of you."

Her smile broadens and she shakes her head. I can't help thinking of what it would be like to live with her and our baby. I've thought about how we could make this work a million times.

"What?" I ask as she continues to smile and shake her head.

"Nothing, I'm glad I'm getting to know the real you—" she cuts off and shakes her head again.

I don't get to ask her what she's thinking as the waitress comes for our order. We place our orders and get into a light banter.

I have to keep reminding myself this isn't an actual date. It feels like one and has all the makings of a perfect date, but we're friends. JC is only showing me all the things I want in my future wife, so I'll know her when she comes along.

Jodie Cadence

"Tell me something I haven't learned about you?" I say as Hershel and I walk from the car back to my place.

"Give me a second to think about that. You know I love to eat. Especially when you're cooking. You've seen how much I read, and you know everything I read isn't for work or study.

"I keep up with all the latest thrillers from my favorites. What haven't I told you about myself? Have I told you that I used to sing in the choir?"

"Nope, I would have remembered that. Really?"

"Yup, Mom had me and Chance in choir from the time we were little. I kept up with it for years."

"Why did you stop?"

"It hasn't been the same without her. Something has been missing. Once I stopped, I couldn't bring myself to return."

I tighten my hold on his arm and snuggle in closer. Feeling safe around Hershel has become so natural. He's growing on me more and more.

"I get it. I used to do these little crafts with my mom. After we lost her, I … I just couldn't anymore."

"That had to be so hard on you and Mel. You guys were so young. Technically, I was a grown man when we lost Mama.

"I couldn't imagine what it would have been like if Chance and I were younger. Pop was so lost and we kind of had to figure things out for ourselves. He meant well, he was doing the best he could, but until Miss Coral came along, he was a shell of himself."

"There isn't any clock you can set on your grief. There are times when I'm still crippled by mine. As a little girl I woke almost every day feeling like someone was pressing a stapler to my heart over and over again.

"Aunt Coral was there to soothe over the pain and help us breathe, so I get how your father must feel to have her in his life. She was our lifeline too."

"Did you ever get back into crafting?"

"No, I've been watching the kids at Children's House make their crafts for sale and I want to jump in, but I'm happy in the kitchen. I don't know if I'll ever craft again."

"Maybe we'll both find our way back."

"Maybe."

We step into my apartment and kick off our shoes. A smile comes to my face as he makes his way to the refrigerator for two beers. He's been bringing beer by to stock my fridge whenever he comes by.

"So do you want to take the test while I'm here. You know, to have me here for emotional support. I'm more than happy to sit with you."

I take the beer he's offering me and shrug my shoulders. Do I want him here with me? Now that he's mentioned it, I sort of do.

"I mean, you're here. I have the tests in the bathroom. I could do it while you're here."

He chuckles lightly. "We should probably stop with these. Look at me, already a bad influence."

I laugh. "As long as you're not handing them to our son for his thirteenth birthday or something."

"Pop would kick my ass for sure."

"What do you think he's going to think about all of this?"

He smiles wistfully. "I think he'll be happy for us. He may need some time to process how we're going about this, but I get a feeling once the baby is here none of that will matter to him."

"I like Jack. I think he's going to make a great grandfather. He's been so kind to us. I think he already sees himself as a father figure to us."

"Oh, you three are his girls whether y'all know it or not. Chance and I have become an afterthought," he says with a smile.

"I love that for the baby. There's so much love he or she will be surrounded by."

"I'm excited for little league or recitals. I'm going to be the loudest, proudest dad there."

I get a pang in my chest. Hershel is starting to sound like he wants this more than I do. The gleam in his eyes tugs at something in me.

I'm starting to see all of this as something we can do together. In fact, at this point, I wouldn't want to do it with anyone else. Hershel makes me feel safe.

He's the friend I didn't know I needed. Some nights I swear he's making love to me and on the verge of blurting out his safe word. Other times, I tell myself that I'm projecting as I fall into my own feelings.

"Then come on, let's see if we're having a baby," I sing as I place the beer down and head for the bathroom.

That's enough time bonding. It might be time for me to head back to the city and allow us to cool things off. Lord knows I'm tired of David and need a break from seeing his ass smiling in my face day in and day out.

Once in the bathroom, I grab the tests I have under the sink. I grab two just to be safe. Hershel stands outside the door looking nervous. I laugh and shake my head.

"Have a seat. I'll pee and then let you know when I'm done."

"Oh, right," he says, then sits down on the floor outside the bathroom door.

He looks so adorable. I don't have the heart to tell him I meant to go sit on the bed or in one of the accent chairs. To be honest, I feel better knowing he's so close.

I close the door but leave a small crack in it as I go to do my business. God, could I pee any louder. Rolling my eyes, I hurry up and finish.

When I'm done, I wash my hands and chew on my lip. My heart is pounding. I can feel the sweat dewing on my lip.

"Hershel," I whisper as my throat tightens.

He comes rushing in and wraps his arms around me. I melt into him as I close my eyes. I shouldn't feel this comfortable in his embrace.

He tucks my head under his chin as he tightens his hold on me. I inhale deeply and slowly open my eyes. The words flashing back at me take my breath away and my knees buckle.

Not pregnant.

"Oh, baby, no, no, no. It's all right," Hershel, coos as he slides down to the floor with me in his arms. "We're not going to give up. This is only the beginning."

"What if I can't? What if we don't?" I can't form a proper sentence to express myself.

He kisses the top of my head. "We can. We will. We're going to do this together.

"I'm not going anywhere. I promise, Jodie. We're going to have a baby.

"I'm going to give this my all. I know we're going to make this happen. I feel it in my gut we're meant to be parents. We're going to have our baby."

I get choked up and can't respond. All I can do is allow him to hold me as I sob in his arms. The last two weeks feel like years. However, I don't have too many years to try.

***

I wake to a sore body and the sound of Hershel's phone buzzing. He's fast asleep beside me with his warm body heating mine. I'd be lying if I said I haven't been getting used to waking in his arms.

He's a cuddler. After sex, he always pulls me into his arms to hold me. Even though sex was different tonight, after was no different. He pulled me right into his chest and tucked my head under his chin as he fell asleep.

I fight not to wonder who's calling him at this time of night. My feelings shouldn't be getting involved in this. However, a tiny voice is telling me to wake him and find out.

His snores grow louder, and my lids become heavy. I snuggle into his warmth and shrug it off.

CHAPTER NINE

Frustration

Hershel

"Have you seen Chance? He's looking for you and he seems pissed," Lauren says as she walks over to me at the desk.

I already have a lot on my mind after last night. JC broke my heart when she fell apart. When I offered to be there for support, I didn't know how much she would need me.

Yeah, I saw Chance calling last night, but I didn't want to leave JC's side. When I woke this morning, I had a ton of voicemails and texts from my brother, but I wasn't in the right headspace to answer them. I'm still not there.

"No, I haven't seen him yet," I mumble.

"You guys have a falling out or something?"

"Hershel, good, you're alive. Now, I can kick your ass," Chance growls as he comes storming my way.

"Not today, bro. It's not a good time," I say before he gets to me.

"I'm going to head to my station," Lauren says and hurries off.

I focus back on the bookings I'd been going through. I have a few more tasks to get through before I need to head in for my shift at Children's House.

I'm on schedule to work a few hours at Paws tonight too. It's a lot but I should be fine. I have the morning off tomorrow.

My mind goes to JC. I want to head to her place to check on her and spend the night after my shift but that might be too late. She's not supposed to be at the house today.

Maybe I'll find time to pop into her office. I just want to hold her in my arms for a little while. Something shifted between us last night.

Sex was way different. I felt a deeper connection with her. I made love to her without trying to hold back.

The best part was that I felt her with me. There was no denying it. She allowed me in, to bond with her.

"Are you even listening to me?" Chance bites out.

"No, I'm not. I told you it isn't a good time."

"What's going on with you? Since when do you leave me hanging with a busted truck? Pop had to come out and help me."

"Since I have shit of my own going on. You know I would have been there if I could have been. I had something I needed to take care of."

"You haven't been yourself lately. Are you finally going to tell me what's going on?"

"Not today."

"Whatever."

I sigh as he storms off. After promising JC I wouldn't tell anyone about us, I don't think I should tell Chance where I was or what was happening when he called.

Trust is the one thing JC and I have that's strong. I'm not going to set us back. An ache starts in my chest, causing me to rub at it.

I pull my phone ready to text JC. However, the device vibrates in my palm as I retrieve it. It's a text from her.

Jodie Cadence: *Thanks.*

The single word holds so much weight. My heart swells with the knowledge that I was there for her, and she allowed it. That's the plan, to continue to be there for her as she needs.

Jodie Cadence

A glance at the clock tells me I've been staring blankly at this computer screen for the last hour. I should be looking over this campaign for Gretta and sending in my approval.

However, I can't stop thinking about last night. I don't know what came over me. We haven't been trying for long, but I just thought it would happen sooner.

My cycle came this morning, and I wanted to puke. I knew what the test said but I was still holding out hope. Hershel was so patient with me.

"Jodie, Dr. Harrington is here to see you," Juile-Ann, my assistant pops her head into my office to say.

I look to the door startled at first. Clearing my throat, I stand and go to head out to see what he's doing here.

A smile comes to my lips as I walk out to find Hershel standing in the lobby with a bouquet of roses in one hand and a basket in the other. I lift a brow as I stop to stand in front of him.

"What's all this?"

He shrugs. "I was thinking about you. I had some time before my shift at Paws, so I stopped by.

Taking the roses, I give them a sniff. They're gorgeous. So vibrant and bright.

"Thank you. This is sweet."

He winks. "I wanted to do something to make you feel better. I got your text about tonight and your situation. I thought you might like a few things to take my place."

I smile wider. I told him he didn't have to drive to Kelly tonight because it's that time of the month. I wasn't excepting him to stop by.

As I glance at the items in the basket he's holding, I see bath salts, an eye mask, chocolate, a candle, and a few other things. I bite my lip. Hershel has proven to be a better boyfriend than my last three and he's not even my boyfriend.

"Well, what do we have here?" David croons as he comes out of his office.

I roll my eyes. This is the last thing I want to deal with. This dude is becoming like that fart you make in the aisle and try to run from before anyone knows it was you, but it travels with you anyway.

"Just dropping somethings off to my baby before I head to work," Hershel says as he leans in and kisses my forehead.

My heart leaps a little as the endearment rolls off his tongue. I don't know why it makes me so giddy inside. He calls me his baby all the time.

It doesn't mean anything. Especially not when he's talking dirty to me. It's his go to.

"So you have more than one job or something? I thought as a doctor you'd be well off. Jodie Cadence, is this really the guy for you?"

"I'm going to stop you there. I've been kind up until this point for the sake of my woman. All bets are off from here on out.

"Jodie doesn't ever have to worry about finances as long as she's with me. I work because I'm a man and I like to keep busy. Money has never been the motiving factor for why I do anything, nor has it needed to be.

"I don't need to lead with my pockets because I bring an emotional IQ of a grown ass man. I know how to mentally stimulate my partner. I have never asked Jodie what she brings to the table because I had it set when she sat down.

"Don't let the pretty looks fool you. Again, I tolerated you but today is not the day. I'm not in the mood and I'm shutting this shit with you down," Hershel growls.

Well, damn. That shit was fire. Hershel has me thinking I'm his woman right now.

He turns to me. "Baby, I'll see you later. I need to get going. Call me if you need anything."

With that, he places the basket down on the front desk and turns to saunter out. I watch him go with a smile on my lips. I like this side of Hershel.

"Ah-at-ah. You heard the man. Not today. Go find something else to do," I sing as I hold my hand up at David when he opens his mouth.

CHAPTER TEN

Not Yet

Jodie Cadence

About two months later …
It's been two months and I'm still not pregnant. Hershel has been there for me each month no matter what. He even offered to come with me to see Dr. Cathrine.

He's been to one session with me. I was reluctant at first, but I think it was good for me. I'm making progress. Progress that's causing me to see Hershel in a new light.

"What do you think about this game night with friends, Chance is planning?" Hershel asks from the kitchen where he's in my fridge.

He closes the door and heads my way with two beers. He's shirtless and barefoot, looking like he belongs here as much as I do. I've gotten used to him in my space.

"I think it's cool as long as everyone is ready to lose to me and my sisters."

He snorts. "I think it's nice of Chance to want Jo to make more friends."

"Ah, I should have known there was an ulterior motive," I sing over the rim of the beer he just gave me.

"How should we play it? David isn't going to be there. Are we going as a couple or just friends?" he asks as he leans in and pecks my lips.

I inhale and sigh heavily. Alice mentioned whispers starting to grow about us. More volunteers have been coming by the Children's House.

Because of David, Hershel and I have been showing affection while at work. Subtle touches and smiles. Enough to make people wonder but not be sure of what's going on.

"I don't know. He's not going to be there, and we don't want to fuel the rumors. I don't want to ruin your chances at a real date with someone you're interested in, you know?"

"Yeah, I get it. We can remain neutral. I wouldn't want to get in the way of you finding a connection either."

"This isn't about to get weird, is it?"

"No, not at all. You ready for bed? I have to leave early in the morning. I have the morning shift."

"Hersh, are we okay?"

"Yeah, baby. We're all good."

My shoulders sag because I know from his tone, we're not. I just don't know if he's catching feelings or if it's something else. He did promise to use his safe word if he does.

He's a big boy. He can speak up for himself. Let it go, Jodie Cadence, let it go.

Hershel

In the two and a half months I've been coming to Kelly to see JC, I've been falling for her. I've tried not to. I've tried to throw up as many walls as she has, but I'm losing the battle.

The more time I spend with her, the more I want to be around her. That sarcasm drives me crazy, but it keeps me on my toes. JC is just easy to love. She's caring and wears her heart on her sleeve even though she tries to cover it up.

"You look like you have something on your mind," Pop says as he and Coral walk into the kitchen.

I didn't sleep over JC's because I needed to give the situation some space. I don't want to say my safe word because I don't want this to end. Telling her how I feel could cause her to walk away.

"I do," I mumble wishing I could have a real talk with my dad like I used to.

"Sounds like you two need some space. I'll head back upstairs."

"No, it's all right. I might benefit from a female perspective."

"Well, what's troubling you, son?"

"I … I. Pop, what if I didn't choose the path that would make me happy? What if now at thirty, I truly know what I want and it's all within reach but everything I want is wrong?"

"Wrong how?"

"I don't think animal medicine is what fulfills me. I'd rather work with children."

"Then I'd say get your laptop. Let's find you a school to get you where you need to be. We're doing great here at the inn. I could afford to hire another hand.

"Why would that be wrong for you? Do you need help with your tuition? I can cover that if you need," Pop says as he wrinkles his brows.

"I have a confession. Mom encouraged me to go back to school for human medicine. I've already completed my studies to become a pediatrician. I'm in my residency right now.

"I thought you wanted me to be a vet to help out here on the ranch. Mom tried to tell me you wouldn't care as long as I was happy.

"Before she died, it was like our little secret. After she was gone, I couldn't bring myself to tell you. I wanted to hold onto that one last thing she and I shared."

Pop swallows hard as his eyes tear up. Coral reaches to rub her hand up and down his back. I don't realize I'm holding my breath until Pop speaks.

"I'm proud of you no matter what you choose to do with your life. You have always been your own person. I never thought you would remain here on the ranch like Chance.

"I'm fine with that. Knowing you have changed courses and finished another degree fills me with so much awe, pride, and joy to be able to call you my son.

"Can I add that there's nothing wrong with change. You often have to change to find what makes you happy. Your favorite meal could be one thing today and something totally different a year from now.

"That doesn't make it wrong. It makes it your preference. Your choice."

"Yeah, but what if what I want and what I choose aren't the same thing as what my future wants? Isn't it selfish of me to keep hope for something someone else has expressed they don't want."

"Ah, I see," Coral says with a knowing smile on her lips.

"I think I do too," Pop chuckles.

"Patience. You are going to have to call on all your patience to climb that wall.

"I'm not saying it's impossible or that you shouldn't try. All I'm saying is patience is the key to that heart. You can't force the lock, and you can't smash the door in.

"Doing either will burn the whole thing down. But if you demonstrate patience and show you're really there, like a kitten getting used to their human, you will find a loyal friend.

"How do I give patience and not harm us both? I … I'm already all in."

Pop rumbles with laughter. "I told you," he says to Coral.

She gives me a warm smile. "Don't be hard on yourself, Hershel. Just have patience. Be yourself and everything else will fall into place. Word of advice. That one opens up best in her places of comfort. The kitchen being one of them."

"Thanks, Miss Coral. I'll keep that in mind."

Coral stands and reaches across the island top to place a hand over mine. "Choosing to fall in love is never wrong, honey. It's how you handle it that weighs for or against you. Just be honest with her and yourself."

With that, she turns to leave me and Pop sitting looking after her. I'm lost in my thoughts as I think their words over. I thought Pop would be angry with me. He took the news about the change in my career and the fact that I've been keeping it a secret from him way better than I thought.

I snap my fingers and turn to look Pop in the eyes. "You knew, didn't you?"

"I did. Your mama told me. I was only waiting on you." He laughs. "I'm so very proud of you, Hersh. Excuse me, Dr. Harrington."

I swallow hard. "Thanks, Pop. I didn't mean—"

"You don't need to explain. I think I understand where you were coming from. Lisa was an amazing mother. We lost her too soon. You wanted to hold onto what you thought was the last of her in your life, but she will always be with you.

"The day you become a father, the day you get engaged, when you marry. She will be with you for all the things. Every time I look into your and Chance's faces, I see her and know she's with me. Those things, those moments, they can never be erased."

I stand and move to pull him into my embrace. Even though I still don't know what to do with all these feelings for JC, I feel lighter. It's probably time I tell her how I feel.

CHAPTER ELEVEN

Caught

Hershel

"I hate that I've been too busy to come to see you," I say against JC's neck as I hold her from behind.

"Hersh, we shouldn't be doing this here," she pants.

"I don't care. I want you and I miss you. It's driving me crazy not to have you," I groan as I cup her breasts over her dress and squeeze.

"Mom asked me to come out here and check on you to see if you needed any help since Chance is busy with the house today. Come on, Hersh, anyone could come out here and catch us."

"Worrying about who catches us when or where isn't going to get us a baby," I growl against her neck as I start to bunch up her dress. "Besides, you knew what you were doing coming out here in this dress."

It's a simple white strapless sundress with yellow motifs all over it. However, it's stunning on her. Her brown skin is begging me to sample it with my tongue. It's been a week since we've been able to meet up at her place in Kelly.

Our schedules have been conflicting. The most we've been able to do is text and talk on the phone. Don't get me wrong, I love our talks.

We've been growing as friends during my late-night shifts when we talk on the phone during my breaks. JC has been as much a support for me as I have been for her.

I lost my first patient, and she came down to the hospital to hold me as I sobbed like a baby in the parking lot. That night we had sex in my truck during my break. It was passionate and soul connecting.

We connected on a different level that night. The look in her eyes made me dare to think there could be more between us. When I come deep inside her, I could only pray that would be the one. That was the last night we were together.

"Hersh, if I let you fuck me, we can't get carried away. It has to be quick before someone finds us."

"Baby, no one comes back here. There's nothing but barrels and beer here with us. Look how wet your pussy is for me already.

"You can't tell me you don't want me," I whisper in her ear as I push her panties aside and push my fingers into her.

"Oh God, yes. I missed you too. I want to feel you deep inside me."

"Fuck, baby, I need to be deep inside you. I've been hard since you walked in here."

"Why are you in here shirtless? Are you trying to make me jealous? Or were you waiting for someone else to show up?"

I growl and tug her panties down her legs then drop my pants and thrust into her. She reaches for the racks in front of her and holds on as we both groan deeply.

I bunch her dress in my palms and use it to guide her back on me with each thrust. I'm so hard right now. I bite my lip as I watch her ass bounce around my cock.

"Fuck yes, I've missed your dick so much. Hershel, please fuck me harder."

"Shit, baby. I don't know how I've gone this long without you. God, you're so wet. You're about to come, aren't you? I can feel it."

"Yes, yes, yes," she cries out.

"*Fuck*," I growl as I come.

"Is someone here?"

I cover JC's mouth as I stifle my own laughter. That sounds like Benny, one of our beer hands. He's not going to come back here if we remain quiet. JC looks up over her shoulder at me in surprise, then narrows her eyes.

I bite back my laughter as I lock eyes with her, then lift my free hand to my lips to shh her. I'm still inside her with a semi-hard erection. However, as she looks back at me and begins to squeeze her walls around me, I begin to grow fully hard once again, not having completely lost my initial arousal.

JC moans around my hand covering her mouth as I begin to thrust slowly. Her brows knit as I continue to move in and out. I nod my head at her confusion to let her know yes, we're still doing this.

Her eyes roll back as I pick up the pace a bit. Moving my lips to her ear, I pant against her skin with each stroke. I grab her waist and groan when she comes around me right as I climax and spill into her.

"That was crazy," she whispers as I slip out of her body and bend to lift my pants back into place.

I then fix her dress and peck her lips. "Nothing like an afternoon break to get you through the day."

"Your freaky ass wanted to get caught," she says as she turns to look at me.

"Wouldn't have bothered me either way." I shrug.

JC yelps as I lift her by the waist and place her on top of the nearest crate. I then snatch up her panties from the floor and stick them in my back pocket. I look around for where I tossed my shirt before she arrived and saunter over to it to tug it back on.

"What are you doing?"

"I'm going to finish up back here. You're going to keep me company like your mama told you to," I croon.

"She told me to see if you needed some help."

"Exactly. This will all go so much smoother with a pretty face around. Humor me.

"Let's talk. It really does help the work to go faster. When I was little Mama would come out here with Pop all the time."

"Did you spend a lot of time out here with him too?"

"Yeah, I did. Once I was old enough to follow the rules and hold a conversation, I'd sit and talk to Pop all the time."

"You have so many fond memories. I think that's what I'm beginning to love about this place. The memories hit different, you know?"

"I'm not sure I follow you."

She lifts her shoulders and sighs. I put down the barrel I'm moving and go to stand between her legs. She pushes my damp hair out of my face.

"Things connect here. The scent of the beer has become a trigger for me. I go to a bar in the city with friends after work and this is the first place to come to mind.

"Certain sounds pull me into thoughts of being here laughing with you, Chance, and my sisters. The connection is … everything has become more tangible. Spring Valley has created roots."

I wrap my arms around her and give a gentle squeeze. I love when we have moments like this. The titles we put on it all don't matter. It's just us talking like we belong together.

"I guess I do get it when you put it that way. I think I took that all for granted in the past. I know I've made some memorable moments in this beerhouse today."

"Oh, hush. You know how to ruin a moment. Get it all out now, tonight you and I need to be on point."

I knit my brows. "What do you mean?"

"Game night is tonight. Remember?"

"Yeah, I remember. I'm helping Mel with the set up."

"Cool, I left some work stuff in Kelly. I need to run to the apartment before tonight. Mel will need the help."

My heart sinks as I realize she's putting up her walls. Then it dawns on me that nothing has truly changed in the last two weeks. I haven't told her about my true feelings so we're not attending tonight as I couple.

I take a step back. "You should head on out. That way you can make it back on time," I murmur.

"Hersh, did I say something wrong?"

"No, I'll finish up here and get on over to help Mel out. You don't want to get caught in the afternoon traffic."

She scoffs. "You call what happens around here traffic?"

"It is for us."

"Hershel, please talk to me."

I peck her lips. "We can talk later tonight."

Before she can say another word, I turn and walk off. I have a lot to think about. I think I'm going to tell her how I feel.

Jodie Cadence

"Okay, anyone know what's the deal with Hershel? There's something different about him. He's always been hot but … I don't know. It's like he has a new confidence or something," one of the women says.

I can't remember her name, but she's been watching Hershel all night. I keep telling myself I have no right to be jealous. I truly don't but I can't help getting a little possessive when I see her or that Lauren chick ogling him.

"Now that you mention it, Margret, I think you're right. Could it be the change over to human medicine?"

"Huh? What do you mean?" Margret says.

"Oh, you haven't heard? He's practicing pediatrics. Isn't that right, JC? He works over at Children's House with you, doesn't he?"

I stand frozen not knowing what to say. Yes, there are rumors floating around town, but I've learned not to listen to them as they are often wrong and these two need to learn to follow suit.

"Oh, honey, come on. I doubt that's it. He has a new swagger about him.

"Like he's been slinging some big dick around and he knows it. Rumors have always been that the mayor and the Harrington boys are packing. Whoever she is she's one lucky bitch. Look at him."

"What are you guys talking about?" Lauren comes over and asks.

Margret and Stella begin to choke on their beer. I can't help the smile that comes to my lips. Serves them right. Old gossiping heifers.

"Nothing, I was just wondering what has gotten into Hershel," Margret says.

"What do you mean?" Lauren asks.

"I think he's excited to make career changes in his life. Margret here thinks it's something else," Stella says.

"Something else like what?" Lauren asks looking nervous.

Margret watches Lauren's reaction and a smug smile comes to her lips. "Something like a new relationship," she purrs.

Lauren's face crumbles. While I hate how she watches Hershel, I'll admit Lauren is sweet. Clearly, she has a crush on Hershel and he's the only one who doesn't see it.

I've had enough of this as the mean girl vibes begin to fill the air. I'm not on that bullshit and I don't want to be around it. Margret is not my cup of tea and Stella might be added to that list soon.

"Lauren, I'm in charge of running the first game. You want to assist me?"

Her eyes light up. "Sure, I'd be happy to help."

***

This has been entertaining, but something has been off with Jo and Chance. Not to mention Hershel has been a bit distant tonight. I know I told him we should act as friends tonight in front of everyone, but this doesn't feel like we're friends at all.

However, I do think I made a friend in Lauren, she has stuck by my side all night. People have started to leave, but she's still here helping me to clean up. Mel is out back with Cash, drinking wine and talking.

I plan to leave them to it. Neither of them knows how to kick back. It's good to see my sister letting her hair down.

"Can I ask you a question?" Lauren says softly, pulling me from my thoughts.

I look at her to find her watching me closely as she chews on her lip. I give her a gentle smile. Lauren is pretty with her green more so hazel eyes and long brown hair.

"Sure, what's up?"

"Is Jo seeing Hershel?" she whispers as her cheeks turn pink.

I burst into laughter. I guess Chance and Jo are doing well keeping things on the low from everyone. However, if you ask me you have to be blind to miss what's going on between the two of them.

"No, she's not seeing him."

"Oh, then it's you," she murmurs as her cheeks redden.

My laughter dies in my throat. I was not expecting that one. I turn away and don't say a word.

Placing a hand on my arm, she causes me to turn my gaze back on her. Although there is sadness in her eyes, she's trying to force a smile. I feel bad for her.

"It's okay. You don't have to say anything. You're gorgeous. I can't blame him."

"It's not what you think. Why haven't you ever told him how you feel?"

She shrugs. "It's never felt like the right thing to do. I'm not that forward and I suck at flirting."

"Close mouths don't get feed."

"See, I could never be like you. I think that's one of the things that has attracted him to you. Hershel loves a challenge and I'm anything but."

"You shouldn't sell yourself so short."

"It's the truth. I've had this stupid crush since high school. I've always known he's out of my league.

"You're really nice though. If I have to watch him fall in love with someone else, you're a great option. Not like all the other women around here who only want him and Chance for their money."

"Thanks for the vote of confidence but like I said, it's not like that and I don't think he's falling in love with me."

"Then you really don't see the way he looks at you."

CHAPTER TWELVE

Special Places

Hershel

JC has had her walls up since game night at Willowbrook. She ignores me at work and hasn't answered my calls when I call to check in before I head to Kelly. I know for a fact she's been spending most nights at Willowbrook.

For that reason, I haven't gone to her place so we can talk or better yet, so we can make a baby. This is frustrating. I have no idea what's going on.

We usually talk things out. However, it's like I'm losing my best friend. I get the feeling Mel knows something is going on between us because she gets this little smirk on her lips when she sees me.

"Hey, you all right?" Chance asks as I sit staring off into space.

"Yeah and no."

"You want to talk about it?"

"Again, yeah, but no."

He snorts and pats me on the shoulder. "I'm here if you need me."

"I mean, I wouldn't know where to start. I don't know what I should or shouldn't say."

"Is this about JC?"

"Bro, you know?"

"You're my older brother. I know you better than anyone. It's not hard to see something is going on between you two."

"Actually, at the moment it's not."

"Can I give you a bit of advice?"

"Go on. I'm open to anything at this point," I huff.

"Jo is the love of my life. She means everything to me. Has she been guarded, yeah.

"But I'm crazy about her and now that I know her reasons, I'm willing to fight that much harder to have her in my life. If JC is the one, don't sit here sulking. Turn on that charm and show her the Hersh I know.

"You're one of the good ones. It's kind of hard not to love you. You have a good heart, and you love hard.

"I've seen it with my own two eyes. You never give up on the ones you love," he says.

"I'm not giving up on her. It's kind of hard to charm someone when they're avoiding you."

Chance rolls his eyes. "Since when has that stopped you?"

I groan and tug a hand down my face. He's right but I haven't come up with a plan yet. I don't want to push too hard, but I don't want to wait until she shuts me out completely either.

Suddenly, it hits me. I snap my fingers as an idea begins to form. I think I know just what to do.

"Can you do me a huge favor?"

"Sure, anything. You know that."

"Give me two hours. JC is at the house. Can you bring her to the lake? Don't tell her where you're taking her or that I'll be there. Just get her to me, please."

"You got it. I'll come up with something."

"Thanks."

***

I'll admit it. I'm a hopeless romantic at heart. If JC were open to dating, this would be something I would set up for us to do often.

However, because we're just friends this should be enough for her to open up to me. This is a special place for me. I want to share it with her.

"What's all this about?" JC asks as she steps out of Chance's truck.

I tip my hat to him in thanks for bringing her here to me. He gives a honk then backs up and turns to leave. JC spins to look at his truck as he speeds away. She then spins on me.

"Before you get angry. I just wanted to talk, and you've been avoiding me."

"So you have your brother kidnap me and bring me here?"

"He didn't kidnap you. He asked you to take a ride with him. At least that's what I asked him to do," I murmur as I rub the back of my neck.

She places her hands on her hips and purses her lips at me. God, I've missed her so much. She looks adorable in the black off the shoulder shirt, jeans, and ballet flats.

"See, this is the weird shit I'm talking about. What do you want, Hershel?"

"Come, sit with me. I hate the way things are."

"What are you talking about? Things are as they should be. I've been busy and haven't had time to ride all the way out to Kelly."

"Jodie, please. I can feel you putting up a wall and pulling away from me. Whatever I've done, I'm sorry. Just tell me what's going on."

"You have nothing to be sorry for. I'm not your girlfriend. You should be out dating while I'm busy so you're not getting attached to me."

"I don't want to date anyone. I don't have time for anyone else in my life. Things have been perfect the way they are. You get me and I enjoy spending time with you. Jodie—"

"Hershel, this is starting to feel so selfish. Maybe it's time I look at the other options. The ones that scare the shit out of me."

"What?"

"I've gone back to the insemination plan. There's still a crazy waitlist at the bank I vetted, but I'm going to make the deposit, and my name will be added."

"Really?" I breathe as I try to keep my legs under me.

"Yes, none of this has been fair to you. I want you to live your life. Date, give the women who want to be with you a chance."

"Wow, I didn't know sleeping with me was so terrible."

"Hershel—"

"No, it's fine. I thought we at least had a friendship happening here. If this is what you want. I'll back off."

She sighs. Then she circles her finger in the air. "All of this—the puppy eyes and pleading words—only works for you. Not even my freaking type," she huffs.

"You say that, but you know more about me than anyone in my life. Admit it, I'm your weird best friend. You miss me too."

She tilts her head to the side with a small smile on her lips. "Fine, I have missed you, you weirdo. Eating lunch in the corner by myself does suck."

"Wait, you've been hiding to eat? That's why I don't see you?"

"Yeah, you're too persistent for me to sit in the cafeteria."

I chuckle in relief and close the distance between us. Cupping the side of her face, I then lean in and take her lips. Thankfully, she opens for me and wraps her arms around my neck.

I dip at the knees and lift her onto my waist, then turn and move over to the blanket I set out for our date. Meanwhile, I devour her lips and groan into her sweet mouth.

As I lower us to the blanket, I break the kiss and place my forehead to hers. The connection is there. I feel it.

JC looks into my eyes, and I swear her walls crumble right before me. I wrap her in my embrace and hold her tight. I'm falling so hard for this woman.

"Are you sure you don't want to date?" she says softly.

I want to blurt out: I do. I want to date you, but I don't think I have that option.

Instead, I say. "Let me feed you. We can talk later."

Jodie Cadence

I have to admit. I was in my feelings after talking to Lauren. The way she watches Hershel, she would know if he's catching feelings or something. Look at how she figured out we've been hooking up.

In the last week, I've been keeping my distance. Especially after Mel called me out on keeping my secret. Thank God for Children's House.

I received a call before she could get the truth out of me. Hershel isn't the only one I've been avoiding. However, I can't say I'm mad at Chance for bringing me out here.

Finding Hershel out here waiting for me pulled at something in my heart. This man has continued to check on me and my feelings. If I'm honest, I think I was pulling away because I'm the one folding.

He's become my place of comfort. I've been missing him, and I'm terrified of doing all this alone. I have my reasons for not wanting to be inseminated.

I have a fear of doctors and medical facilities. I have since my mother started in and out of doctor's offices and hospitals only to die in a hospital. It's the last hurtle I need to get over with Dr. Catherine in case I can't have an at home birth.

This is the one detail I haven't shared with Hershel. It took everything in me to go through with the checkups to begin this process. Then I found out about my condition. A fact that hasn't helped at all.

However, Hershel makes me feel like I can do this. With him I can conquer it all. The fears, the trauma, I can beat them.

"This has been nice," I say as Hershel begins to pack up the basket that had our food.

"I'm glad you liked it. This place is special to me."

"Oh really? I didn't know there was a lake on the property. This place is so peaceful."

"This is one of three, but this is the one we all come to. It's special to us as a family."

"Am I the first woman you've brought here?"

"You are. I've never brought a girlfriend here."

I frown and tilt my head to the side. He locks eyes with me and reaches to brush his thumbs against my frowning lips. I search his gaze for a beat.

"What?"

"You made the distinction of not bringing a girlfriend here. I'm not your girlfriend, by the way. Anyway, you just spoke a half truth."

He sighs and leans into peck my lips. "You're a female and you're my friend. Anyway." He rolls his eyes.

"I want you to trust me some day. My mother … I used to come here with my mother.

"It was her favorite spot. She brought us here as little boys and when we got older, we would come out here to sit with her. You are the only other woman I have ever been here with."

I lower my gaze to the blanket beneath us. "Trust is something I've been working on in therapy. Before my mother died, I caught my father with another woman.

"I was so young and confused. I never said anything because I thought my mother deserved to heal in peace. I didn't know she wasn't going to heal."

I swipe at my tears. "That was the last time I saw him. He didn't show up after that. He made promises and we waited but he never came back.

"Then there was David's betrayal. I don't want to spend my life this jaded. I think this baggage is what has kept me in toxic relationship after toxic relationship.

"You don't deserve to pay for my father or David's actions. I do trust you—"

He crushes my lips, cutting off my words. I whimper into his mouth and tangle my fingers into his hair. Leaning into me, he causes me to fall onto my back.

My body blooms for him effortlessly. The deeper he kisses me, the more I want to be near him. If you would have told me that I would fall for this man when I first arrived in Spring Valley, I would have said you were crazy.

Now, I'm falling fast and hard. This evening has been sweet and romantic. As he peels me from my clothes and removes his then sinks into me, I know I'm too far gone to stop these feelings.

"Hershel, yes."

"You can trust me, Jodie. I'm here for you. I always want to be here for you. I'm your person."

CHAPTER THIRTEEN

Perfect Love

Hershel

Two years and three months later …

As I stand at my brother's wedding reception, looking across the barn, I have an ache in the pit of my stomach. JC and I have been trying for almost three years for her to have a baby.

That look she gets in her eyes every month guts me each time. We're both healthy other than her condition. However, we have yet to conceive. Watching her with April in her arms picks at the wound festering in my heart.

I want that to be our baby. We're at the end of the line. Our time is almost up.

"You look like you have a lot on your mind?" Pop says as he comes to stand beside me.

"As always but I'm not going to burden you with any of it, not tonight. This night belongs to Chance and Jo."

"I'm your father. My ears are always available. I told you earlier that I'm a master at multi-tasking. What's going on?"

I sigh. "Not here, Pop. Maybe I'll stop by later."

"And ruin my night with my wife. I think the hell not."

"What happened to your ear always being available," I snort.

"Some moments are off limits. We're still technically newlyweds." He chuckles. "Let's take a walk."

"Okay, fine."

Taking one last glance at JC, I then turn and follow Pop outside the barn. This place truly has been transformed. I'm happy for my brother and his family.

"What's going on, son. I've noticed you haven't been yourself lately. Everything all right with the residency?"

"Everything is fine with work. Things have felt much better now that I've resigned from Paws."

"I can see that, but something has still been weighing on you. The contractor called last week. They break ground on the house in a few weeks. Are you nervous about that?"

"No, Jodie and I have been fine in the apartment we've been sharing in town. We're right next to Children's House and Shelby's."

"Ah, this is about JC."

I sigh. "Yeah, Pop it is. I know she finally told Coral about her condition and what all that means. We're running out of time and she's still not pregnant.

"I … I feel sick about it. If only you knew how hard I worked to be the one to do this with her and I'm failing. I've been to my doctor to see if I'm the problem but I'm not.

"The last thing I want to do is place this in her lap, but if I say nothing and she doesn't at least get a checkup to find out what can be done, that's going to haunt me," I explain.

"I see. Women can be difficult to know how to navigate. Especially with topics like this.

"However, I've watched you and JC build a bond like none other. My suggestion would be to talk to her. Gently tell her your concern. Offer to be there with her no matter what and let her figure things out from there."

"What if … Pop, I love her. I know we weren't supposed to catch feelings but she's my world. Not just the woman I want to have a baby with, but she's my best friend.

"I haven't told her because I don't want to lose her. I'm ready to propose but I don't know if she's there. Jodie is so hard to … I don't know.

"I can't say she's hard to read because I know her better than anyone else. I guess what I'm trying to say is that when it comes to me, I don't know what she's thinking," I think aloud.

"I say you do what you've been doing, Hersh. Talk to her. Be as honest as you can be.

"You two have been sneaking around for almost three years. You might have come clean six months ago, but we knew."

"I'm sorry, Pop. I wanted to be fully honest, but I didn't want to break her trust. It wasn't my secret to tell."

"I get it. Listen, son. I love you and I'm proud of you no matter what. It breaks my heart to know what you two have been carrying all this time.

"JC is a fighter and she's strong. I truly believe in my heart that if anyone can come out on the other side of this, it would be the two of you. Don't give up."

"Thanks, Pop. I needed to hear that more than you know."

He pats me on the back. "Come on, I think they're playing my song."

Jodie Cadence

"That was a time," I say as Hershel and I walk into our apartment.

Jo and Chance's wedding was everything. I'm so happy for them. April is so precious and Jo is pregnant again.

I would be lying if I said my heart didn't ache as I held April in my arms. I couldn't help wondering if I'm just not meant to have a baby of my own.

Hershel walks up behind me and wraps his arms around me. I melt into him and soak him in. We've been living together in an apartment in Spring Valley for the last six months.

My lease was up in Kelly, and it made more sense to move here. Especially since I haven't gotten pregnant and we wanted to double our efforts. Not to mention I now own Shelby's.

Living with Hersh feels as natural as breathing. He's become my rock.

"It was a wonderful wedding. I've never seen my little brother so happy in my life."

He sounds a bit off, so I turn in his arms. Looking up into his blue eyes, I search them. Seeing the shutters come down right before me, I bristle.

"Are you all right?"

"I think we should talk."

"Okay."

He takes me by the hand and leads me over to the couch. As we sit, I try to run through all the things he might want to talk about. Other than me not having a baby, things have been good.

I cook and clean and he takes care of eighty percent of the bills. His idea, not mine. I bought Shelby's and hired Lauren of all people to help me run the place.

She's smart and a fast learner. The repairs will be complete in another five months. That's when I'll be saying goodbye to Caring Hearts.

Next week will be the big fundraiser for Children's House. Some of the art the children have prepared is expectational. The recital before the auction has sold out.

"Jodie, I've been thinking. I'm starting to get concerned about us not having a baby yet. I … I feel like it's my fault you're not accomplishing your dream."

"What? How could this be your fault?"

"I talked you into choosing me to do this with and—"

"Hershel, shut your face. This is not on you. I knew from the beginning that it wouldn't be an easy task."

"Yeah, but shouldn't we be looking at options? Have you spoken with your doctor? We're getting down to the wire."

I jerk my head back and frown. No, I haven't gone back. All that woman is going to do is tell me how small my chances are and how fast my window is closing.

I'm not about to put myself through all that anxiety just to hear what I already know. However, Hershel wouldn't know this. Dr. Catherine works from her home, I feel comfortable going there, not like if she worked in a medical facility.

Seeing the genuine concern in his eyes softens my heart. This man only cares that I get my baby. How can I fault him for that?

I take a deep breath. "Okay, I hear you. I'll make an appointment for this week."

"Do you want me to come with you? I can clear my schedule whenever you need me."

"Look at you. Get to your third year and start sounding like you run things. I'll be fine."

He purses his lips. "I want to be with you. This is important to me."

I palm the side of his face. "I know it is. It's important to me too. I'll make the appointment and get back to you. If you can come with me, that's great, if not, that's fine too."

I don't tell him I'm freaking out inside. I'm doing all I can not to have a panic attack in front of him. Just the thought of making an appointment to go to that office snatches my breath away.

"Baby, I'm here. We're going to do this together."

I'm seconds away from telling him that I've folded. How can he be this invested in my wants and dreams? Yet he's been here for almost three years.

He comes with me to therapy, he spends time with me outside of our arrangement, and he shows me he cares all the time. However, I'm not ready to admit that my feelings have run deeper than I thought they ever could.

"Jodie," he calls me out of my thoughts, causing me to look him in the eyes. "My views have been clouded for a while.

"You don't have to say anything, but I need to get this off my chest. I got us a two bedroom to give you your space, but I always want to be next to you.

"You're all I think about. I … Clouded Views, baby."

I sit blinking at him. I want to respond but I can't. It's like my brain shuts down on me and I'm lost for words.

He leans in and pecks my lips. "I have an early shift I couldn't get out of at the hospital in Kelly. I'll see you in the morning."

With that, he gets up and heads to his bedroom. I sit with my brows knitted. He usually spends the night in my bed.

A tear slips down my cheek. I want to call after him and explain how I feel about him. However, I can't find a single word or the function to speak. Why is this so hard for me?

CHAPTER FOURTEEN

Move Forward

Jodie Cadence

I desperately need to move forward. I've tried to make an appointment to see my GYN three times today alone. The way I start to hyperventilate each time is crazy to me.

I want this baby. Why can't I make this call? On top of that, my head is all messed up over Hershel's words.

I should have been able to tell him how I feel. I'm a straight shooter. I always say what I feel.

None of this is what I want and it's not like me, so here I am at Dr. Catherine's office after work to sort all my shit out. I can't keep going like this. I'll be thirty-three and I'm still arrested by my past.

"I want to be free. I want out of this cage. I should have been able to say something.

"I do care about him. He's become my person. Why is this so hard?"

"Jodie Cadence, first I need you to breathe. It's not uncommon to know what you want and still be afraid to latch onto it.

"You've made so much progress. I want you to remember something you said to me a few months back. I'm not sure if you were even conscious of your words," Dr. Catherine says.

"What did I say?"

"You said. Love brings healing. It stuck out to me because you said it with so much conviction. Do you remember those words?"

"Yes, I do. Mom and Jo have proved them to be true," I say.

She taps her pen against her lip as she studies me. "Yes, but do you feel those words apply to you?"

I think for a moment. "Well, I guess when I think about it. Mom and Uncle Ralph poured so much love into me and Mel. If not for them, I don't think I would have grown into a functioning adult.

"It was one thing to lose my mother, but I felt like I lost my father too. Well, before mom died, he broke my trust. I was so confused and angry.

"At thirteen, I caught my father dicking down a woman I watched smile in my mother's face. Do you know what kind of position that put me in? I couldn't say a word to anyone.

"I felt voiceless after my mother died and I said nothing. I've carried that guilt and hurt for all this time. Almost twenty years. No wonder I'm so fucking broken and can't have a baby of my own."

Tears run down my face as I try to get it all out. I need to move forward with my life before this all consumes me. I choke back a sob as it all becomes so overwhelming.

"I … I feel like all that guilt and anger is twisted up in my womb. Taking up any space a baby would need to be in there. Do you know he tried to blame my mom's illness?

"When he chased after me, after I saw them, he said he only stepped out because she was too ill to be a wife. He needed someone to comfort him. That was bullshit.

"I was thirteen, not five. I remembered the fights and what they were about. He was always a piece of shit. He didn't deserve her.

"But he lied to my face making me feel so small. To be honest, I wanted to believe him. I needed to, but he didn't care. We weren't enough for him to care about," I sob.

"Jodie, I think you're right. Love does heal. For twenty years, you have been healing. However, with healing comes knowing when to let go.

"You're blaming yourself for things that were totally out of your control. It was the adult in the situation who was responsible for the accountability, not you. I want to do an exercise with you.

"It's time for thirteen-year-old Jodie Cadence to leave that hospital and all the hurt living inside of it behind. I think because you spent so much time there and then lost your mother there, it's become an anchor in your present life.

"I believe Hershel represents all the good things you want for yourself, but that anchor has silenced your voice. Today we're going to collapse that anchor. It's time to set you free.

"Then we can ask what's next after a broken heart is healed? Are you ready?"

"Yes, please. This is long overdue."

CHAPTER FIFTEEN

For Spite

Hershel

"Hey, Juile-Ann, how's it going? How's Fluffy doing?" I say as I walk up to the reception desk at JC's office.

"Hey, Dr. Harrington. Fluffy is doing great. Loving his new diet and that dog park you sponsored.

"I'm doing great too. Hanging in there. I'm sorry but Miss Marks isn't in right now."

"No problem. I figured as much. Big night coming up."

"Everyone is so excited. Jodie Cadence put so much work into everything. I can't wait to see the results of her hard work."

"Our hard work," David croons as he comes out front.

I roll my eyes and clench my fists. I'm already frustrated today. It's been a week, and JC hasn't mentioned when her appointment is scheduled for. On top of that, I have to deal with this guy.

David will be leaving Spring Valley now that the fundraiser is happening this weekend. I will be the first to say good riddance. He has been a pain in my ass for far too long.

Juile-Ann clears her throat and pulls a face. We both know Jodie Cadence has done all the work while this asshole has taken the credit. Ignoring him, I get to what I came here for.

"I just wanted to drop off my schedule for the next month for Jodie. You can let her know that I'll do my best to make myself available whenever she makes the appointment for."

"Appointment? What appointment?" Daivd asks as he comes to the desk.

"None of your business," I snap.

"Jodie Cadence is my business. You don't think I buy this bullshit relationship between you two. If you were dating Jodie, you would have proposed by now. She wouldn't have had it any other way," he says smugly.

"Say whatever you want. Once Jodie confirms the pregnancy, I plan to propose," I say just to get under his skin.

Jodie is going to kick my ass, but this guy presses all my buttons and has for the last two and a half years. I already know his fiancée broke up with him.

He has been trying to dig a wedge between me and Jodie ever since. I get this sour feeling in my stomach as a gleam comes to his eyes. It's the total opposite of the reaction I'm looking for.

"Bingo, I knew I was right. You're not dating Jodie. If you were, you would know she has a phobia when it comes to going to any type of medical facility.

"I know your cornball ass isn't here talking about an appointment for a doctor. A baby," he snorts.

He then pauses as he looks me over with a shit eating grin that comes to his face. I'm not schooling my reaction well. Surprise is written all over my face.

"You can't bullshit a bullshitter, my guy. I've just been waiting for you two to slip up. I knew the time would come."

"And JC still doesn't want you so what do you think you're going to accomplish from here?" I bite out.

"I'm going to take my girl back. This project is over and I'm going back to the city. JC will be right with me so I can give her everything she wants and more."

The thought of Jodie leaving with him cuts deeper than I care to admit. I've been counting down the days until he's gone but the thought of her leaving too is unbearable. Jodie has roots here. This is her home.

"I wouldn't be so sure about that."

"What do you think she wants more? Some lie or the man she spent seven years of her life loving, planning with, and actually fucking. I know Jodie in ways you never will."

If I didn't hear my pop and mama in my ear, I would knock him on his ass. However, someone should act like an adult and show Jodie some respect.

"We'll see who she chooses," I say not feeling as confident as I sound.

I'm still processing his words about JC's fear. Clearly, he does know things I don't. I haven't had time to think about how that makes me feel.

"It will always be me. The man who can relate to her experience, who understands her. Not some cracker who only wants her for his bed whore."

The voices in my head go silent and I blackout. When I come back to myself, JC is standing in the lobby with her mouth open. The security guard from next door has ahold of me and David is on his ass.

"There he is. The real savage. I'm going to press charges and sue your ass," David says smugly.

"Shut up, David before I let him finish the job," JC snaps.

I narrow my eyes at her. She looks back at me questioningly. I have to ask because I need to know.

"I came to find out about the appointment. You can text me later unless he's right and you haven't made an appointment because you're afraid."

She closes her eyes and the color drains from her face. I don't need to hear anything else. I have my answer.

I tug from the guard's hold and shove him off me. I then storm out. My anger consumes me.

We're supposed to be in this together, why wouldn't she tell me something like this? I might not be her man, but this is something I should know. Trust goes both ways.

Jodie Cadence

My heart is breaking as I watch Hershel storm out. He doesn't understand. I haven't gotten to tell him what's going on.

He's been on call since my session with Dr. Catherine. I've been trying to wait for a time where we can sit face to face and have a talk.

I had planned to make the appointment this afternoon after I got done with the final details for the fundraiser. I'm ready to take the next steps into my future. Hershel is a big part of that—at least he was.

"Did someone call the cops?" David says while still sitting on the floor.

I turn to glare at him. "Whatever you said, you must have deserved it. That man is the sweetest, most patient, and gentle man I know."

"Ask Juile-Ann, she saw it all."

"Did I? Are you sure? I did take my contacts out during my break. I can't say that I saw anything. Darn seasonal allergies."

"So you didn't hear anything either?"

"Nope. I think my ears cut off in shock after you called Miss Marks a bed whore for a cracker. We don't do things around here like that. Forgive my delicate ears for protecting themselves," Juile-Ann says innocently.

"You said what?" I growl.

"None of that matters. I know you guys aren't really a thing. He doesn't know you like I do. He's not the one, Jodie. You can stop pretending."

How did I never catch that before? He has an accent. It's slipping at the moment.

All this time he's been posing as a Black American. That is when he's not acting uppity and kissing white ass. This is so wild.

I know what I learned about him, but I never reconciled the facts until now. So much is starting to make more sense. He's nothing but a poser.

"You motherfucking—" I cut off and take a calming breath. "You know nothing about me. What you're going to do is get your ass up, find some ice for that knot and black eye, then you're going to go pack up your shit to leave Spring Valley the moment the auction is over.

"Don't not pass go. Don't try to collect a damn thing, just get your shit and go."

"Jodie, come on, baby. I've been here all this time trying to show you I've changed. Don't blow up a good thing."

I scoff. "You've been here covering your ass. Hiding out here so no one in the main office can see you've always been a slacker, hiding behind my talent and hard work. You have only shown me the big ass bullet I dodged.

"Changed. You haven't changed a thing but your drawers. After seeing that ass whipping you just took, you might need to change them now.

"Read my lips, you prick. It is over. I don't want you. If you come near me or my man again, I'll be the one pressing harassment charges and getting a restraining order. Do you understand?"

"Jodie, I—"

"Do. You. Understand?"

"Fine, but you will come crawling back after he's done playing with you. Don't think I'm going to be around waiting."

"He's still talking. Did he forget I carry or is he just looking to give me a reason? I said goodbye," I growl.

He pouts like a child and climbs to his feet. All I can do is shake my head. I march into my office and close the door behind me.

I close my eyes as I lean against the door then I burst into laughter. Hershel was whipping that ass when I arrived. I had to go next door to get Ernie to come help me pull him off David.

"Oh, my God," I breathe as I wipe at my tears and try to quiet my laughter.

"Damn, Hersh," I chuckle and bite my lips.

That shit was sexy. I did not see that coming. Now how do I fix this?

CHAPTER SIXTEEN

In My Feelings

Hershel

The kids all did amazing tonight. I placed a bid on a few of the art pieces. It was the least I could do.

However, I think it's time I head out. My mind has been stuck on my conversation with JC earlier. I wish there were a way she could explain away my hurt.

I just don't think that's possible. The trust is gone. The wound is too fresh.

"You're leaving?" Mel asks as I head for the door.

"Yeah, I have some things to take care of."

"You're trying to pack your things while she's here. I know you're angry, but you should hear her out."

I frown. When JC pulled me aside before the recital, I thought I could talk things out with her, but my anger only returned. Seeing David turned my anger into rage.

I've been avoiding JC since. It's been two days since I've last been to the apartment. I wish I could say it's work that's kept me away, but it isn't. I've been too angry to be around JC.

I'm questioning everything. I want someone in my life who loves me as much as I love them. Jodie has worked hard on herself, but I have no promises that she'll ever see me as I see her.

David's words have been haunting me day and night. I can't get them out of my head. *It will always be me. The man who can relate to her experience, who understands her.*

What if he's right? Isn't that the reason she didn't want me as the father of her child? Jodie doesn't want me because of the one thing I can't change.

Even if David was wrong, she didn't confide in me about something that plays a huge roll in our end goal. Heck, in my life. I'm going to be a doctor.

This could mean that my future wife would never be able to bring herself to come to my place of work. It makes me think she hasn't ever seen me as more than a donor. How can I look at her, knowing how much I love her for her? If only she could love me the same.

"I think it's best. We tried. I couldn't be what she wanted.

"I let my feelings get involved. I shouldn't have. It's best I move on and let her find what she's looking for."

"Are you going to move back into the Inn?"

I sigh heavily. "I was offered a new opportunity to finish my residency in the city. It might be time I changed more than my career path. I don't know if there's anything left here in Spring Valley for me."

"Hersh, I think you're letting your anger talk. You've become family. I hate to hear you sound so hurt.

"My sister has been through a lot. You are the first man I've seen her open up to. She's happy when she's with you.

"Maybe give it a few weeks before you make any major decisions. I'm sure when things cool off, you will see she's closer to where you are than you think," Mel pleads.

"I can't. I don't recognize the man in the mirror anymore. This is for the best."

"You keep saying that, but your face is saying something else."

"I love your sister. That's not going to change for a long time, but … I want to be good enough. I want her love.

"I shouldn't have to change who I am for that. Not when I give all of me and more. I've been single for so long because I don't bend. However, I've been bending for her in every direction. JC doesn't need me to take charge, and she doesn't want me to either.

"We just don't fit. As her friend, I'm leaving. I'll see you around." With that, I lean in and kiss her cheek.

I've made up my mind, I'm moving out. I've already paid the rent at the apartment for the next six months. I even covered the bills. It's up to Jodie what she wants to do with the place.

She's not the only one who needs to heal. I've been broken since I lost my mother. It's time I look at things and find my way back to who I am once again.

Jodie Cadence

"This project turned out phenomenal. You exceeded the financial goal— and the exposure for the town—the data is awe-inspiring," Gretta sings as she pulls me into a hug.

"I can't believe we brought in so much money. 3.8 million from the auction alone. Mr. Copeland's friend from the gallery in the city has already offered to showcase of few of the artists as soon as we can work out the guardianship details."

"Yes, I heard. Rumor is there has been interest in the adoption of a few of the children. You did great, Jodie Cadence. I can see your labor of love shining through."

I give her a big smile. Gretta knows David is full of shit. Her last in person visit exposed a lot. She's been giving him rope to hang himself since.

"Well, you've done a great thing here. I can't wait to see what else you have in mind. This event made the press, and Mr. Copeland is very pleased."

"About that, um."

"Oh no, I was afraid this was coming. You're leaving us, aren't you?"

"Yes, I think it's time. I want to be here with my family. This is my home."

She sighs. "I get it. This place does have it's charm. I'm in love with that B&B you recommended. My husband has been talking about the brewery all night. He can't wait to check it out tomorrow."

I smile. "I'll let Jack know to take special care of you guys."

I pause and take a settling breath as my stomach begins to roll. It's been such a long week. I think my body has reached its limit.

I can't wait to get home and get out of this dress and these heels. I don't think I ate enough today either. I had to make sure everything was right.

"Are you all right, dear? You look a little peaked."

I wave her off. "I'm fine. It's just been a long day."

"Where's David, shouldn't he be helping with the clean up?"

"Your guess is as good as mine."

She purses her lips and frowns. I say nothing because when I make David pay, it's going to be petty ass fuck. I don't want to get him fired just yet.

I meant what I said earlier. I'm not done with that smug prick. I'm going make him to pay.

"Hey, sis. You need any help?" Mel asks as she, Mom, and Jo appear.

"You guys are lifesavers. I have a checklist over there of all the things I need to do before I leave."

"We're on it," Mom says. "Why don't you have a seat?"

"I can't." I shake my head. "I need—"

I rush to the nearest trash can before I can get the words out. What little food I did get to eat today all comes up. I kick my heels off as I hold onto the sides of the trash can and rock from side to side.

Mom comes over and holds my hair back. I look into her eyes as tears burn the backs of mine. Her eyes soften and she smiles back at me.

"I knew you could do it. You're going to be a wonderful mother," she whispers.

I knit my brows, then do the math in my head. I should have started my cycle a few days ago. I thought it hadn't come because of all the stress.

"We did it?" I say in a small voice, sounding more like a little girl than the grown woman I am.

"Yes, my baby. I believe you did."

I clench the sides of the can, not wanting to get my hopes up. Then it hits me. It still may be too late.

CHAPTER SEVENTEEN

Petty As Fuck

Jodie Cadence

I'm petty on a good day, so imagine how petty I can be while pregnant and frustrated because I haven't spoken to the father of my child. The more I think about what David did, the more I want him to pay.

All I needed was a few hours. A few more hours and I would have made that appointment and had Hershel by my side as I overcame my fear. Dr. Catherine is amazing.

I was able to go to my first appointment with the support of my sisters and mom. It wasn't easy, but I got through it. I was able to let the past go and take care of me.

It's that strength I've been calling on as it feels like I have a hole in my heart. Since Hershel refuses to come back to Spring Valley, I'm here in the city to do the only thing I can for now. I'm going to make David's life hell.

"Hey, Miss Marks, it's so good to see you. We miss your face around here," Ben, the doorman to the apartment building I used to live in with David says.

"It's good to see you too, Ben. How's the wife and kids?"

"They're doing great. The boy has started travel ball. My little girls are dancing their hearts out. Can't complain one bit."

"That's great. Listen, I'm going to ask you for a favor," I say and dig a wad of cash out of my bag. "Take this as a gift for all you've done for me when I lived here. Then forget you saw me here today, please."

"Sure, ma'am. No problem." He nods.

See my mom has always taught us to be kind to everyone. The janitor, the restroom attendant, the valet, everyone deserves respect and kindness. I know for a fact the staff in this building can't stand David.

If he were kinder, he wouldn't have to worry about the key I never returned or how I'm about to fuck his whole life up. With a smile on my lips, I saunter my ass right in with a dog carrier in my hand.

Mind you, the property has a strict no pets policy. I ride up to the condo we used to share and let myself right in. I laugh as I push into the apartment.

David should have changed the locks by now. Dumb ass. I guess he's going to learn today.

First, I head to the kitchen and place the pound of fish I bought into the fridge. Then, I unplug the refrigerator and tuck the cord out of reach.

I dust my hands off and straighten once I'm done.

"That's going to stink," I snicker to myself.

With a smile, I grab the carrier with Ace. The cute pug I just spent two hours feeding before giving him a puppy safe laxative. A gentle cleanse for his little tummy.

I then make my way to the bedroom. As I step into the closet I snort. This man and his suits. I note the ones hanging for Darryl the building concierge to pick up to drop off at the cleaners as he does once a week.

A wicked grin comes to my lips. I place the carrier down then grab a piece of David's note pad he leaves instructions for the cleaners on. I then scribble a note for the tailor to take all the suit pants in and lift all the hems by four inches.

Looking at my watch, I see I need to get Ace into place. Like a woman on a mission, I run through the closet knocking every suit, shirt, tie, pairs of shoes, and everything else to the floor.

"Hey, cutie. You want to explore?" I coo to Ace as I open the carrier door.

He comes right out. I lead him over to the piles of clothes where he makes himself comfortable. Then I pat the top of his head.

"Don't worry. When your job is done. I promise a friend is coming to get you and take you to your new home.

"Then we'll get you potty trained. For now, you handle your business. Okay?"

He looks up at me and farts. Or should I say sharts. I laugh and turn to leave.

Pulling my phone as I exit the apartment, I go to make a call to property management. We can't have David breaking the rules, now can we? Not at all.

"Oh, hey, Darryl. Let me grab the dry cleaning for you," I croon as Darryl is walking in as I leave.

"Hey, Miss Marks. Good to see you. I didn't know you were back."

I pull out another wad of cash and wink at him. "I'm not and as far as you're concerned, you never saw me, right?"

He winks. "I haven't received a thanks or a tip since you've been gone. Can't remember the last time I saw you either."

"Great."

I double back to the closet and find Ace tearing shit up. He has chewed through several pairs of shoes and it looks like he's pissed on a pile of shirts.

"Good, boy," I coo as I grab the suits for the dry cleaning.

I hand Darryl the dry cleaning as we walk to the elevator. He has a huge smile on his face as we ride down. That tip will go a long way.

"Hello, yes, I want to report my neighbor in 1027. I believe he has a pet on the premises."

Darryl looks at me with wide eyes. I wink at him. He stifles a laugh.

"Are you sure, ma'am?"

"Oh yes, I saw a dog enter the unit. I was as shocked as you sound. I specifically chose this building due to the strict no pet policy. My allergies and all, you know."

"We will have this looked into immediately. I'm so sorry ma'am. Which unit did you say you're in?"

"Hello, hello. Oh darn, I think I lost you when I stepped into the elevator."

"Ma'am, I'm still here. Hello?"

"Hello? Ugh."

I hang up snickering. Darryl is practically doubled over in laughter. Tears are running down his cheeks. I tip my imaginary hat at him and step off the elevator.

And to think, I'm just getting started. If fuck around and find out was a person, that would be me. Hello.

Hershel

I was able to pack my things and be gone before Jodie got in from the fundraiser that night. Wanting to make a clean break, I decided not to move into the inn. I found a place in Kelly to give myself time to think.

I decided against the job in the city. The more I thought of being that far away from home the more it didn't feel right. The last three months have flown by and I'm miserable.

"You look miserable, bro. You haven't thought about calling her?" Kordell asks as we sit in my apartment drinking beer.

I lean back into the couch and take a sip of my beer. It tastes like nothing. These days nothing taste like anything.

I'm just going through the motions at this point. I haven't figured out how to make this right or move forward.

"Yeah, I have but I don't think I have a right to. Sure, I'm pissed at her, but I did the one thing she was afraid I would. I abandoned her. It's been three months."

I've gone over this in my mind a million times. However, I can't keep sacrificing myself for a love I'm never going to have. I'm sorry things didn't work out but I'm holding to my guns on this.

All JC had to do was be honest with me. I would have been understanding. I would have found a way around her fears so we could have what we wanted.

"Then go home. She's back at Willowbrook, isn't she?" Kordell says, blasting through my thoughts.

"From what Chance says, yeah."

I rub the back of my neck. Chance and Pop have tried to get me back home. They think I need it for closure. I'm not there yet.

"Then what's stopping you?"

"I can't keep doing this. It's not me. Yeah, I'm always the first to help but I've never put myself last like this."

Kordell sighs and slides forward in his seat. He places his beer down on the coffee table and turns to look at me. I finish my beer to get ready for what's coming.

"You haven't been yourself since your mama died but you were happy with Jodie Cadence. I started to see the real you again. She gave you a sense of purpose.

"I feel like you were sacrificing out of love. So what you didn't call all the shots. JC kept you focused on your goals.

"Dude, the path you took with your residency wasn't the easier one. Out of the four in our class who took that option, you're the only one who made it through. And you took almost two years to leave Paws." He pauses to shake his head.

Glancing into my lap, I can't help thinking about how much I enjoyed my time at Children's House. I still call in to check on the kids. I just haven't had the time to go back in person.

I miss working there, but leaving was for the best. Ariel and Corey are still there. Apparently, they both have turned down the families who wanted them. Of all the kids, I grew attached to those two the most.

Pulling a hand down his face, Kordell then continues. "I know you can be determined and stubborn when you have your mind set on something, but JC played a big part in getting you through. As a friend, as a lover, as your person, she got you through.

"You said so all the time when we talked. Trust me, I remember because I was envious of that while trying to get through myself. It's not easy. I'm proud of you, my friend."

I snort. "I'm not the one who's going into pediatric surgery. I'm in awe of you, man."

He chuckles. "Nice. Way to deflect. You know I'm right."

"Well, this has honestly been my first day to myself in months. I'm not avoiding home just because of JC. There have been a lot of third year dropouts."

Kordell groans and sits back, looking up at the ceiling. "Tell me about it. So many have folded under the pressure. I was sure if they made it to their third, they would be good. I mean, you're three quarters of the way through. Why stop now?"

I freeze. His words feel like he's talking about more than work. JC and I put three years into this. Why am I giving up on her now? I swallow down the bile that raises in my throat.

"Maybe my feelings have nothing to do with JC but they're all about how I know I'm failing her," I murmur.

Kordell turns his brown eyes on me. He looks confused for a moment. "How so?"

"I didn't give her a baby. I couldn't be what she needed. I pushed my way in and shit the bed."

"Don't do that. I think a conversation will get you two back on track. You're a great guy, Hersh.

"One of the best I know. Jodie Cadence knows this too. I promise you she does."

"Knowing something and accepting it are two very different things."

He snorts. "I see we're going with stubborn Hershel this round. Okay, next topic. I didn't come here to bang my head against a wall," he chuckles.

CHAPTER EIGHTEEN

Nothing Is Right

David

I have never been this pissed off in my life. I can't stand dogs. Especially those ugly little pugs. The fact that I lost my condo because of one of them and the little fucker defecated all over all my shit makes me hate them even more.

I wanted to punt kick his little ugly ass across the room when I saw him. Imagine my surprise when Danielle, my ex-fiancée came to pick his little ass up and thanked me for dog sitting for her. I haven't spoken to Danielle in over two years.

I wanted to strangle her, but it dawned on me the next day that she isn't smart enough for some shit like this. As I picked up my dry cleaning the next morning for an important meeting at the office—since all my belongings except for the ones on my back were ruined—I learned the real monster I was facing.

I got back to the hotel I was forced to stay in because of the rancid stench throughout my place and tried to get dressed for work. All of my pants were too tight and fit like a pair of Steve Urkel pants.

As I tried on suit after suit and looked into the mirror, one thing became clear. This was Jodie Cadence. She's the only one who could pull off something so diabolical.

When I couldn't purchase a new suit for work because my cards had been locked and frozen due to fraud, I knew for a fact it was her. Jodie has connections in the hacker world and a few connections with some AI guys. This shit was child's play for her.

Not only did I have to arrive at work looking like a fucking idiot, but I was also late for one of the most important meetings of my career. The Spring Valley project had launched my career into pay dirt.

One of our billionaire donors hired Caring Hearts to launch a project for him and I was to take the lead. However, that didn't happen. Instead, I was cuffed and escorted off the property for skimming money off the books.

Did I take the money? Yeah, here and there I had taken some but not the numbers they were talking. Again, all the signs of Jodie Candence ruining my life.

"Hey, pretty boy. You still here?" This motherfucker croons.

While all the other inmates stroll by and mind their business. This motherfucker keeps fucking with me. Now I remember why I hated high school.

It wasn't bad enough that I had just come over from Nigeria with a heavy accent and clothes that were hand-me-downs from my cousins who had already been here. I was bullied for years.

That is until I reinvented myself. I lost the accent and became as Americanized as I could. I immersed myself in the Black American experience. I vowed I would never fall so low again.

Yet here I sit. As hard as I fought to become Americanized, it all has fallen apart. Jodie Cadence was the best and worst thing to happen to me.

"Damn, you smell good," this bastard says in my ear as he comes up behind me. "I heard some rumors about you. I came to see if they're true."

"Back. Off," I hiss.

"Nah, that ain't gonna happen. You see, you weren't dropped in here by accident. You fucked with my little cousin and now I'm going to fuck with you, playboy."

I close my eyes and fight back the tears. I took one million of the four million I'm being charged for. I don't deserve this.

CHAPTER NINETEEN

Visiting Hours

Hershel

Two months later ...

For the past five months, I've been in Kelly licking my wounds. Kordell gave me a lot to think about during his visit. However, I haven't had the time to face any of it.

Pop is always trying to get me to come by the ranch, but I truly have been too busy. With my third year has come a lot more responsibility.

"Hey, handsome. Did you think about my offer?" Miss Hollis purrs as she comes over to me while I look over a chart for one of my patients.

Jane Hollis is the mother of a little girl who comes in for iron treatments. Angel is adorable. However, her mother has been relentless.

In the last two months, I've started to move forward but I'm not in a place to date yet. I still get ready to text JC at least five times a day if not more. I miss her.

I don't think I'll be ready for a relationship for a long time. Not to mention, this guilt that's been riding my back. I abandoned her just like she thought I would.

I have so much I want to say to her. I've been doing research on her condition, trying to find a way to solve her problem. I still don't have answers.

I also have a ton of questions I would need answered to dive deeper. Questions I no longer feel I have a right to ask. Pushing my thoughts aside, I grin at Miss Hollis.

"I don't really have time to date and I'm not really in the head space to, if I'm honest. But thank you for the offer. It was kind of you."

She places a hand on my chest and looks up into my eyes. I should have known she wouldn't let it go easily. Frustrated, I glance over her head in disinterest.

"It's only dinner. I promise it will be a good time."

I open my mouth to reply but close it as I narrow my eyes. I swear I'm hallucinating. There's no way JC is here.

She wouldn't come into a hospital. Better yet, why would she need to be here in mine? I have to be seeing things.

I don't snap out of my shock until everyone between us seems to move out of the way. Her back is to me now as she rushes in the opposite direction.

However, I know it's her. The hair and the charm bracelet I gave her for Christmas give her away. I'm in motion before I can tell my legs to stop.

"Jodie," I call after her. I then say to Miss Hollis. "Excuse, I need to go."

I rush after JC as fast as I can. I bite out a curse as I miss the elevator she climbs into. I race for the stairs instead. When I get to the lobby and push out of the staircase, I see her racing for the front doors.

Picking up the pace, I catch her just before she gets to the exit. I grab her arm and call her name. She turns to look up at me with tears in her eyes.

My gaze drops to her protruding belly, and my knees nearly give out. I'm stunned and confused for a moment. Then a million questions run through my brain.

Did she go through with the insemination? Did she go back to Meet and Breed to find someone else? Was David right?

Did she go back to him? She looks to be pretty far along. Does that mean she didn't stop to think about me?

Jodie Cadence

In the beginning I wanted to give him the space he clearly needed. Getting home to find his things gone from the apartment nearly crumbled me. Everything I wanted was within reach.

Yet it was all slipping away because of an asshole. I have never hated anyone the way I hate David. All I've been able to think about for the last five months is that we did it and Hershel hasn't known a thing.

Jack and Chance have been working on him, but he hasn't come home to Spring Valley. Not even once. I came here today because I want him to at least know.

He should be aware of the gift he has given me. I can only hope we find our way back, but he'll at least know the truth.

"Are you happy?" he asks as he keeps his eyes on my belly.

"No, I miss my best friend."

He finally looks up at me. He nods and takes a step back. I want to reach for him, but I can barely breathe.

"I'm sorry," he murmurs. "It looks like you were right from the beginning. I wasn't the one. If I had stayed, you wouldn't have gotten what you wanted."

I look down at my stomach and place my palms against it. Then it hits me. He doesn't realize I'm carrying his children.

"Hershel, you have nothing to be sorry for. You gave me everything I wanted and more. You're my person.

"I folded the moment I woke to you staring at me in my sleep like a weirdo. You had that goofy smile on your lips and you looked like you would do anything to get by my walls if I allowed it."

"I would have."

"Would have or still will because I don't want to raise our children by myself. You promised you'd be there to help me."

He looks at me confused for a beat. Then the light bulb goes off. He moves closer and palms my stomach.

"You're pregnant by me?"

I nod. He cups the side of my face and kisses me passionately. I wrap my arms around his neck and hold on tight.

"I love you," we say at the same time as he breaks the kiss.

We both laugh as he pecks my lips repeatedly. I melt into him as he rubs his nose against mine. I finally feel whole again.

"Are you all right? Is being here too much?"

"That's what I wanted to explain. Dr. Catherine and I worked through that fear so I could go to the appointment with you. I just hadn't had the time to with everything else going on.

"David needed to mind his own damn business. I hated that I couldn't tell you I loved you when you told me you had feelings for me. I froze.

"Between that and my fear of making that appointment, I had to do something, and I did. I couldn't allow my past to rob me. Not when I was head over heels for your weird ass."

He kisses my forehead. "Wait, you said babies? Did I hear you right?"

"Yup, we're having twins. I guess God is blessing us for our patience."

His jaw works as he looks to be holding back tears. Then he fist pumps the air and lets out a shout, causing everyone in the lobby to turn and look at us.

He then wraps his arms around me and hugs me tight. "I fucking love you, baby," he says into my neck.

I run my fingers through his hair. "I love you too."

"Listen, I need to head back up, but I want to see you after my shift. Here, take my keys. You can hang at my place.

"I just had groceries delivered. I'll text you the address," he says and pulls his keys to hand to me.

"I'll be there."

He kisses me hard then turns to walk off whistling. I shake my head with a smile on my face. Damn, he looks good in his scrubs.

CHAPTER TWENTY

Together Again

Hershel

That had to be the longest shift of my life. Knowing Jodie Cadence has been in my place all day and I couldn't just leave to be here with her, was killing me.

A smile comes to my lips as I see her duffel bag by the front door when I walk into my apartment. The way I rushed home after my shift, I'm surprised I didn't get pulled over. I'm going to be a dad.

I haven't stopped smiling since learning we're pregnant. Finding out Jodie is carrying twins was a bonus I never expected. However, I'm over the moon about it.

My smile grows as the scent of something delicious fills the air. Damn, I missed this woman's cooking. I head to the kitchen and find a plate in the warmer waiting for me just like she used to do for me.

My mind fills with all the times JC has taken care of me. I was wrong. This is Jodie's love language.

Cooking and taking care of me was her way of showing me she cared. I'm smiling so hard as I take the plate to the table. I can hear the shower running in the bathroom.

I scoff down the food so I can go and join her. I'm already growing hard as I think of how sexy she looked at the hospital earlier. Her body has changed in so many ways.

Her hips, her ass, she looks great carrying my children. She was glowing. I couldn't be happier right now.

Music begins to play in the bedroom as I place my dishes in the dishwasher. "F***in Wit Me" by Tank spills through the speakers. I chuckle.

I guess I'm not the only one who's thinking about the time we need to make up. As I walk toward the bedroom, I pull my shirt over my head. My jeans are the next thing to go.

When I step into the bedroom, Jodie is sitting on the bed in a cute little black nightie. I lick my lips as I allow my gaze to run over her. I nod my head toward the bathroom.

"I'm going to shower. I'll be right back."

"Did you find the food I left for you?"

"Yeah, it was amazing. Thanks, baby."

"You're welcome. Take your time. I'm not going anywhere."

My nostrils flare as she rubs her belly and slightly parts her legs for me. Without another word, I turn and rush into the bathroom naked.

Hoping into the shower, I make quick work of washing the day away. I use the bodywash Jodie loves then wash my hair. When I'm done, I wrap my waist in a towel and head back into the bedroom.

This time "God Went Crazy" by Teddy Swims is playing. I couldn't agree more. God made something special when he made this woman right here.

I was made for her, and she was made for me. I've been hers since the first time I saw her. There isn't a day where she hasn't owned me.

"I've missed you so much," she says as I come into view.

She's now on my side of the bed on her knees as she looks back at me lustfully. Her breasts look so much fuller. Her belly is so adorable on her.

Moving to stand in front of her, I palm her face and lean in to take her lips. She moans into my mouth and reaches to tug my towel off.

I deepen the kiss as I go to place a knee on the bed beside her. However, she has other plans. She reaches for my hard cock and wraps her hand around it.

Jodie then shifts on the bed to sit on the edge, then leans in to take me into her mouth. I groan and throw my head back. She pulls away and makes a slurping sound. I look down and find her looking back at me through her lashes.

"Fuck, baby, that feels so good," I say as I watch her stroke me.

Not taking her eyes off me, she takes me back into her mouth and starts to bob her head as she gets me nice and wet. She begins to reach behind her. That's when I notice the bottle of oil she's reaching for.

Once she has it in her hand, she snaps it open and begins to pour it down my stomach, letting it drip down onto the base of my shaft and down to my balls, then using her hand to spread it over my length.

"Mm," she moans as she takes me deeper.

I reach for her hair and hold it back as she works me with her mouth. Widening my stance, I pump my hips into her face. I groan from deep as my toes curl.

"God, I've missed you. That's so good, baby. You know me so well.

"I love that fucking mouth. Keep sucking me like that. I'm going to give you just what you're looking for, baby," I says tightly.

She grabs my balls and wraps her hand around them and my base as she lifts me to allow her saliva to dip down me. It's the gentle stroking and massaging that's going to get me there.

"I thought you were happy to see me, Hersh. Come on, baby. Show me," she purrs as saliva drips down her face and onto her breasts.

"Oh, baby, you don't have to ask me twice," I growl as I stroke myself with one hand and grasp her throat with the other.

I begin to feed her my length, holding her in place as I move in and out of her mouth. Feeling my orgasm rush me. I release her and take a step back.

Swiftly, I gently push her onto her back and drop to my knees. Placing her legs over my shoulders, I then begin to play with her pussy with my hands. She's always been sensitive to my touch, but this is well beyond that tonight.

Her moaning and panting turns me on. I have her dripping wet, and I haven't even started to eat her pussy yet. When I do lean in and begin to blow on her soft skin, she bucks off the bed.

"You like that, baby. I haven't touched you yet, but you're so fucking wet. You want me to eat this juicy pussy?"

"Well, duh. I'm waiting for you to eat it then beat it up. Come on, Hersh.

"It's been too long. I miss you. Give me that big, fat dick. I need it," she cries out.

I dive in and eat her pussy like I'll never get a chance to again. She tastes different but I like it. I hum into her core and add my hands into the mix.

After I make her come a few times, I get up and guide my way into her tight core as her ass hangs off the edge of the bed. I'm careful with her as I take the brunt of her weight.

Locking her thigh against my chest I keep thrusting in and out of her. I can't help but groan when her wet pussy creams all over me as she clenches her walls around me.

"Yes, yes. Damn that shit feels so good," she says breathlessly. "Mm, don't stop."

"I've got you, baby. I can feel you about to come. Give it to me.

"I want to feel you come for me. You're so wet," I croon as I wipe sweat from my face with my forearm.

"Oh shit, *fuck*," she screams.

This time I can't hold back as her climax hits and she starts to milk me with her tight walls. My hot seed shoots into her. I groan and give one final thrust, holding my hips against her until I stop pulsing and twitching inside her.

When I pull out, I climb onto the bed beside her and try to catch my breath. Jodie turns her head to look at me and smiles. She reaches for my face and palms my cheek.

"I love you," she says, causing my heart to swell.

I turn my face and kiss her palm, then place my hand over her stomach and tug her gently toward me. Looking into her eyes, I see her love for me.

"I love you too."

Jodie Cadence

After Hershel gave me his keys, I drove back to Spring Valley to pack some things to stay over. When I returned and got to his place, I decided to make him dinner. Then I spent the rest of the day waiting for him.

Now I can barely keep my eyes open, but I don't want to fall asleep. I've missed Hersh so much. Having his arms around me now has left me feeling safer than I have in months.

"Do you know what we're having?"

"No, I came today to let you know about the pregnancy and invite you to my next appointment. That's when I plan to find out their genders."

He kisses my bare shoulder. "God, I'm so excited. I love you so much. I'm sorry about abandoning you."

"No, I'm sorry I didn't tell you about my phobia. We didn't have to lose any of that time, but I get why you were upset."

"I feel like such an asshole. If I ever see David again, I'm going to knock him on his ass again."

I snort a laugh. "You don't have to worry about that. I don't think we're ever going to hear from him again."

"What aren't you telling me?"

"Nothing," I sing as I grin. "Are we going to build the house?"

He chuckles. "I called the contractor while I was at work. They can break ground and get things rolling next week. Although, I think we should look at the plans and make a few adjustments."

"What kind of adjustments?"

"For one, I don't think we need to build a buddy house. There doesn't need to be your side and my side, we're going to be a family. I was also thinking of having an office at home to see patients once I have my license."

"Is that right? You think I'm going to shack up with you because you knocked me up."

I begin to giggle as he tickles me. I gasp as I feel the babies move. It's not the first time, but I'm still getting used to it.

"Are you okay?" Hershel asks anxiously.

"Yes, I'm fine. I think they're moving. I felt a little flutter."

"This is so surreal," he says in awe.

Then he moves to speak against my stomach. I roll onto my back to give him better access. He palms the sides and looks up at me with a smile.

"I think we should vote on it, guys. All in favor of Mommy and Daddy building a house for the four of us, make some noise."

I laugh as I feel the flutters again. "Um, I can't be sure they both moved. I don't know about this vote."

"Everyone who wants Daddy to marry Mommy, do a little wiggle."

This man begins to wiggle his big body as my children flutter in my womb as if they understand what he's talking about. I laugh and wipe at my tears.

"It's settled. We're building a house and I'm going to propose. Jodie Cadence Harrington. It has a nice ring to it," he croons.

"That it does. Um, do you mind if I ask you about something?"

"You know you can talk to me about anything."

"I still go to Children's House to see the kids. There are quite a few who have found a home and families. I worry about Corey and Ariel.

"They haven't been open to any of the families who were interested. I was thinking about adopting them myself, if they'll have me. I know it will be a lot with Shelby's and the babies, but I know I can make it work."

I chew on my lower lip as I wait for him to reply. A smile comes to his face. His eyes light up.

"I think that's a great idea. Those two have a special place in my heart. I say we go for a visit and see if they'll have us. We can go through the process from there."

"Have I told you I love you?"

"Yes, but I'm still getting used to hearing it so keep going."

I crook my finger for him to come to me. He crawls up my body and kisses me passionately. I cup his face.

"I love you, I love you, I love you," I sing.

CHAPTER TWENTY-ONE

Our New Life

Hershel

I finally have a day off and can go home to Spring Valley with Jodie. She's been with me since the day she arrived to tell me about our babies. I love coming home to her.

My life has been lighter with her around. When I spoke to Pop, he sounded so excited for his new grandchildren. I realized he was trying to tell me without telling me all along.

I wasn't surprised when he said he would be throwing a cookout this weekend. Jodie and I decided we would do the gender reveal at the barbeque with all the family there.

"Are you ready for this?" I ask as we pull up in front of Children's House.

We wanted to come here before we head to the ranch. Corey and Ariel know we're coming to see them today. However, we didn't tell them for what other than the fact that we're taking them to the ranch for the cookout.

"Yes, I'm nervous. Do you think they're going to want us?"

"I think they're the perfect addition to our family. I'm sure they'll be excited to consider us as their parents."

"I'll be crushed if they don't want us, but I'll understand. When you're waiting for your person nothing else feels right until they arrive."

I lift her hand to my lips and kiss the back of it. I know she's talking about how she feels about us. Our connection has grown in the last few weeks.

Going to her appointment to find out the sex of the babies was a huge turning point for us. I got to see first-hand the trauma she's been dealing with and how hard she works to be able to walk into a medical facility.

Being able to be there for her was a gift. To think Jodie had planned to do all of this on her own. She was ready to take this on against all odds.

If that doesn't show her strength, I don't know what does. These two children we created and the two inside Children's House will be lucky to have her.

"I don't think we have anything to worry about. Come on, let's get in there."

I climb from JC's car we drove here in and grab the tube with the plans to our new home. I then go to open her door and help her out. She looks so pretty in the soft pink dress she's wearing.

We head inside hand in hand. Ariel's little brown face is the first one to come into view. She's smiling from ear to ear.

"Corey, they're here. Come on," she calls out.

The light sound of the piano stops and a few seconds later Corey comes running. I can't help but smile as I note the two are dressed up. Corey is in a pair of khaki shorts and a crisp blue button up with shiny black shoes. Ariel has on a pretty yellow dress and little sandals on her feet.

However, I also notice when both their smiles fall when they take in Jodie's full belly. It's like the light goes out of their eyes. The disappointment in Corey's little blue eyes rings clear.

Tears well up in Ariel's eyes as she looks between us. I smile and squat down.

"Hey you two. We thought we could all hang out and talk before heading to the ranch for the celebration," I say.

"Okay," they say sadly as they link their fingers together.

We all head to the game room where Jodie and I asked to have time to meet with Corey and Ariel. The kids are walking ahead of us as they try to whisper to each other without us hearing. My heart aches as I catch their conversation.

"They're not here for us. They already have a baby. You were wrong," Corey says.

"I know but I didn't make this one up in my head. They're the ones we prayed for. The ones we've been waiting for.

"Pastor Gray said all it takes is a mustard seed of faith. And he said if two or three agree it's done. That's why we joined as a team.

"You're my best friend. The Lord took my family, so I'd find you and them. I'm not giving up.

"They're ours. We can help with the baby. I don't need much love. What they have given me is already enough.

"Have faith, Corey. They'll want us. Keep praying."

"Lord, hear our prayer," Corey starts.

From the tightening of Jodie's grip on my hand as a lump forms in my throat, I know she has heard every word as well. I look to her and see the tears swimming in her eyes. I nod at her answering her unspoken words.

Pastor Gray runs the local church the children go to on Sundays. It's clear Ariel has taken to his teachings. I make a mental note to make sure that's something we keep up with as a family.

"Cupcakes," Ariel squeals excitedly.

She rushes to sit down at the table set up with cupcakes and finger sandwiches for us. Then as if remembering her goal, she freezes and stands back up. My heart aches.

"Please sit," Jodie says. "This is all for you guys."

Ariel gives a small tentative smile. Corey moves to her side, and they sit together. Jodie and I sit across from them. Jodie places a cupcake and two sandwiches on each of their plates.

"I know you like turkey, Corey. But you prefer chicken, Ariel so I sent over each of your preferences. Green flags are turkey. Orange flags are chicken."

"These are so good," Ariel sings as she nibbles on a sandwich.

"Don't fill up too much, there'll be plenty of food at the cookout. If you guys still want to come after we talk," I say.

"Are you here to ask me to paint the baby when it's born?" Ariel whispers.

"If you want me to compose a lullaby for them, I will," Corey says.

"You are both so sweet and we would love that but that's not why we're here," Jodie says.

"Then why are you here?" Corey asks.

"Come here," I say and wave the two over to one of the square tables. I pull the plans from the tube and spread them out on the tabletop. The kids climb onto stools and peer down at the plans in confusion.

"Miss Jodie and I are building a house for after we get married and when the babies arrive," I say.

"Babies?" Ariel gasps as her face becomes crestfallen.

"Yes, we're having twins. This right here will be the nursey. When they get older, this will become one of their rooms. We came to ask you guys which rooms you would like to call your own. If you don't see a square that looks right, let me know, we'll create a space just for you."

"For us?" Corey says with wide eyes.

"Yes, if you will have us. Dr. Harrington and I strongly believe you two will complete our family," Jodie says as she comes over and runs a hand over Ariel's hair and place the other on Corey's shoulder.

"Yes, we want to come with you. Can we pack our things today?" Corey says with a beaming smile.

JC and I chuckle. "We still have a lot of paperwork and building to do but they are putting a rush on things for us. You'll be able to come to our temporary home for a trail run by the end of the month," Jodie says.

"Once you guys decide on your rooms, I'll get the final plans over to the builder. Our home should be ready by the time all the paperwork and things go through."

"I'll be stopping by to spend time with you guys as much as I can until we can take you home," Jodie promises.

"I told you we needed to keep praying. They do want us. Yes, we'd love for you to be our family. Is this room available for me?" Ariel asks pointing to one of the bedrooms.

"Yes, that can be all yours."

"I'd like to be where I can still play and not disturb anyone," Corey says.

"How about this room?" I ask and point.

"Yes, please, Dad," he says and looks at me cautiously.

"You got it, son. Let's finish our snack so we can head to the ranch with the rest of our family. We're all finding out if you're going to have brothers or sisters."

Ariel jumps up and wraps her little arms around me. I lower to embrace her. Her little body is trembling.

"God heard my prayers. I knew from the day you arrived you would be my dad. I've just been waiting for Miss Jodie to fall in love with you so you could come and get me," she whispers.

"Sorry we took so long but we're here now. I promise we have more love to give, darlin'."

"Mom, when will we get to meet the babies?" Corey asks.

"They'll be here soon," Jodie chuckles.

"I can't wait," Ariel sings.

I stand and place a hand on Jodie Cadence's back. I can see she's getting emotional. I kiss her lips and flex my fingers against her back.

We finally have our family.

Jodie Cadence

As we stand in the backyard of the inn, I can't help smiling. This place is filled with so much love. You would never know my family and I were transplants.

I smile wider as I look across the yard at Uncle Ralph and Jack playing with the kids. I shake my head as I think of how my own father missed out.

"I'm so happy for you, " Jo sings.

"Thanks, I had to do something to help my man keep up with his younger brother," I tease.

"Right, because my husband is determined to keep me pregnant."

"Like you're complaining," Mel laughs.

"I guess you're right. Between you and mom, I hardly see my first born. Sometimes I forget April is mine," Jo laughs.

"I will not be shamed for spoiling my niece. She loves her Tee-Tee, and her Tee-Tee loves her. You're not about to come between us," Mel says and puts on a pout.

I laugh at my sisters. April isn't short of any attention. She's been bouncing between her grandfathers since I arrived. She has Uncle Ralph and Jack wrapped around her tiny finger.

"You girls are going to wish you savored the days when you had all the help you could stand. They grow up so fast. One minute you're wishing you could shield them from everything in the world.

"The next they have their own little humans to protect and mold. It all happened too fast, and you can't turn back time to do it again no matter how much you wish you could," Mom says.

"Cause Lord knows you needed to start fresh with these two," Mel says.

I roll my eyes at my sister. She has some nerve. She's no saint.

I glance over by the grill and find Hershel talking to Chance and Cash as they all laugh and sip beer. This is so far from the way we grew up. This life is so peaceful.

"Lauren is really working out at Shelby's, isn't she," Mom says.

"Yeah, I feel bad. I might be overworking her."

"Are you kidding me? She loves it. I thought she was going to quit working here, but she's committed to both."

"Yeah, I see that. She's a fast learner and I love that she refuses to cut corners. It helps me release the reigns a lot easier."

I have had to lean on Lauren with Shelby's. Opening the kitchen for dining services was a bigger undertaking than I was expecting. People really love my food.

For now, we only open for lunch and dinner twice a week. In a year or two, I might add on a few days as we're always busy on those two days. Alice still hasn't retired like she had planned to do.

I think having me and Lauren there has given her a second wind. That or she just can't let go. I'm thinking it's a bit of both.

"Mama, Mama," Ariel calls as she comes barreling toward me with a huge smile on her face.

She wraps her arms around my neck excitedly. Hearing her call me that so easily fills my heart with joy. She's been using the name since she first tested it out.

"Grandpa Jack said when we move into the temporary house, I can have a room all to myself for painting. And after we move into our house, I can keep it for when I visit him and grandma."

I can't help but smile. Mom and Jack have offered for us to stay with them at Willowbrook until our house is done. Hershel thinks it's a great idea since I'll be due soon and he works in Kelly for now.

I'm sort of excited about it. This is my first pregnancy and having mom around makes me feel better. Jack being a devoted grandfather only helps that much more.

"Oh, I know just the room too," mom says with a big smile.

"Can Auntie Mel take you shopping for supplies?" Mel asks as she runs a hand over Ariel's hair.

"Really?"

"Of course, you can pick anything you want. I've got you."

"Thank you. I look forward to it, Auntie Mel."

She hugs my sister then takes off again. Mom comes and wraps an arm around me. I look at her and smile. She has this proud look on her face.

"I'm so proud of you. What you're doing for those two on top of having my grandson and granddaughter, I know my sister is smiling down on you with such a full heart.

"I love you, Jodie Cadence. I'm so proud of the woman you've become. You deserve all the happiness in the world."

"Thanks, Mom. My mother left me and my sister in capable hands. I couldn't have asked for a better guardian. I only want to give that back to those sweet children."

"Hey, baby," Hershel croons as he comes over to me.

I look up and he pecks my lips. He's been smiling like crazy since the gender reveal. I haven't been able to stop smiling either.

Today has been amazing. I feel like life is clicking into place for me.

"Hey, you."

"Come dance with me. I miss having you in my arms."

"We were just dancing two songs ago."

He winks at me. "A moment without you near me is an eternity too long. Humor your fiancé," he says with a smile.

I glance down at my ring. I had no idea he was going to propose tonight. It was perfect in a Hershel way.

"Come on, I might have one more dance in me just for you."

"That's my girl."

EPILOGUE

Nightmares

Mel

I thrash about, fighting my demons. Trying my best to keep them at bay. Something is tugging at me, shaking me.

"Baby, wake up. You're safe. Baby, come back to me.

"Wake up. It's just a dream. I'm right here.

"Mel, babe, wake up. Nothing can hurt you. I'm here."

I wake and pop up in bed. I'm drenched in sweat and disoriented at first. Then I realize I was dreaming again.

It's the same nightmare all the time. That same night keeps haunting me over and over again. This isn't right, I should be free.

"Baby, are you all right?"

"No," I murmur.

I turn my face into his neck and inhale before breaking down into sobs. I hate that I can't shake these stupid nightmares.

"I'm here. I've got you."

"Why can't I stop having these nightmares?"

"I don't know, baby. You know it was him or me. I hate that you had to, but you made the right decision.

"A few seconds later and you wouldn't have this burden. It would have been mine. There isn't a day that goes by that I don't wish it had been."

He rubs my back to sooth me as I continue to cry. I know I did what I had to do, but it still haunts me. It's like I've become trapped in a cycle.

I don't know who I am anymore. My life has turned, and I missed where my exit is. I should be happy, but I'm dealing with this instead.

"This too shall pass. I'm here for you."

"Why can't I let this go?"

"Because taking a human life isn't easy. But I swear, I'm here to get you through this. You will get through this."

ABOUT THE AUTHOR

Blue Saffire, award-winning, bestselling author of over eighty contemporary romance novels and novellas, writes with the intention to touch the heart and the mind. Blue hooks, weaves, and loops multiple series, keeping you engaged in her worlds. Blue writes for her own publishing company, Perceptive Illusions as Blue Saffire, as well as Royal Blue.

Blue and her husband live in a house filled with laughter and creativity in Long Island, NY. Both working hard to build the Blue brand and cultivate their love for the arts. Creative is their family affair.

Blue holds an MBA in Marketing and Project Management, as well as an MED in Instructional Technology and Curriculum Design. She is also an NLP Master Practitioner.

ACKNOWLEDGMENTS

Another palette cleanser. This book was fun, and it gave my brain a rest to unlock some other things. Not to mention I realized how petty I can be. LOL.

One more book and the Spring Valley world will be complete. Mel will bring more drama and laughter for sure. We also get back to Courtland and his mess. I can't wait.

My dear reader friends, I can't go without saying thank you so much for your continued support and patience. This year is paying off as I focus on what's in front of me and not the whole picture at once.

Thank you for the encouraging reviews, emails, videos, posts, shares, comments, and DMs. Big thanks, friends. Remember, sharing is caring. If you have a friend who reads, let them know about me, please and thank you. Shout out to those who already let me know they have.

To my husband. Don't fear my petty. You're good and safe. ROTF. I've never heard you laugh at one of my characters so hard. LOL. Thanks for reading.

Never forgotten but always to be mentioned. Thank you, Lord. I thank you for teaching me and ordering my steps. Thanks for bringing me back to the main thing.

Blessed and highly favored. To God be all the Glory.

Next! What's going on, Mel? Well … we will find out soon.

Wait, there is more to come! You can stay updated with my latest releases, learn more about me, the author, and be a part of contests by subscribing to my newsletter at

www.BlueSaffire.com

If you enjoyed *Clouded Views*, I'd love to hear

your thoughts and please feel free to leave a

review on my website. And when you do, please let me

know by emailing me TheBlueSaffire@gmail.com

or leave a comment on Facebook https://www.facebook.com/BlueSaffireDiaries or Twitter @TheBlueSaffire

Other books by Blue Saffire

Placed in Best Reading Order

Also available …

Legally Bound

Legally Bound 2: Against the Law

Legally Bound 3: His Law

Perfect for Me

Hush 1: Family Secrets

Ballers: His Game

Brothers Black 1: Wyatt the Heartbreaker

Legally Bound 4: Allegations of Love

Hush 2: Slow Burn

Legally Bound 5.0: Sam

Yours 1: Losing My Innocence

Yours 2: Experience Gained

Yours 3: Life Mastered

Ballers 2: His Final Play

Legally Bound 5.1: Tasha Illegal Dealings

Brothers Black 2: Noah

Legally Bound 5.2: Camille

Legally Bound 5.3 & 5.4 Special Edition

Where the Pieces Fall

Legally Bound 5.5: Legally Unbound

Brothers Black 4: Braxton the Charmer

Broken Soldier

Brothers Black 5: Felix the Watcher

A Home for Christmas

Doctor Feel Good

Brothers Black 6: Ryan the Joker

Brothers Black 7: Johnathan the Fixer

Wild Hearts

Pieces of Trevor's Heart

Ballers 3: His Team

Ronan Book 1: Kings of New York

Dylan Book 2: Kings of New York

Brooklyn Book 3: Kings of New York Series

Coming Soon…
King of Gods Book 4: Immortal Iron Brothers Series
King of Past Book 5: Immortal Iron Brothers Series

Other Blue Saffire Series

Hold On To Me Series
My Funny Valentine
Be My Valentine

Hitter Squad Series
Remember Me

Work Husband Series
Unexpected Lovers
My Best Friend's Wish
The Ones Left Behind
The Last Ones Standing

The Lost Souls MC Series
Forever
Never
Always

The Moran Brothers Series
Love Notes
Stay With Me

The Ahole Club Series**
Pit Book 1: The A**hole Club
Ox Book 5: The A**hole Club
Kelex Book 6: The A**hole Club

Immortal Iron Brothers Series
King of Knights Book 1
King of Inferno Book 2
King of Tides Book 3

Touchdown (Standalone)

Check out Blue Saffire exclusives on the
BlueSaffire.com website

The Fixer
His Miracle Baby

Dark Disciples Series
Razor
Dane
Trip

Discipline Disciples Series
Wounded
12 Rounds

Bay Breezes Series
Professor Jones
Room 112

Love's Brew Series
Heart to Heart
Beer With Me
Clouded Views
Home is Here coming soon …

Other books from Evei Lattimore Collection Books by Blue Saffire
Black Bella 1

Destiny 1: Life Decisions
Destiny 2: Decisions of the Next Generation
Destiny 3 coming soon…

Star

Other books from Royal Blue Gay Romance Collection written by Blue Saffire
Kyle's Reveal
Beau's Redemption

www.ingramcontent.com/pod-product-compliance
Lightning Source LLC
LaVergne TN
LVHW020047110826
845155LV00029B/664

* 9 7 8 1 9 4 1 9 2 4 4 0 2 *